THE GILDED CAGE

King George III could not bear to part with his daughters when they reached marriageable age. The Princess Royal escaped the paternal stranglehold at the age of thirty-one, when she married the Duke of Würtemberg. Her sisters were not so fortunate, and desperation drove them to form unsuitable attachments. The young Princess Charlotte, only child of George, Prince of Wales, made fun of her 'maiden' aunts, until she too became the victim of an eccentric father.

Books by Freda M. Long
in the Linford Romance Library:

THE DRESSMAKER
THE SOLDIER'S WOMAN

FREDA M. LONG

THE GILDED CAGE

Complete and Unabridged

LINFORD
Leicester

First published in Great Britain in 1974 by
Robert Hale Limited
London

First Linford Edition
published 1999
by arrangement with
Robert Hale Limited
London

British Library CIP Data

Long, Freda M. (Freda Margaret), *1932 –*
The gilded cage.—Large print ed.—
Linford romance library
1. Love stories
2. Large type books
I. Title
823.9'14 [F]

ISBN 0–7089–5549–5

Published by
F. A. Thorpe (Publishing) Ltd.
Anstey, Leicestershire

Set by Words & Graphics Ltd.
Anstey, Leicestershire
Printed and bound in Great Britain by
T. J. International Ltd., Padstow, Cornwall

This book is printed on acid-free paper

Principal Characters

King George III.
Queen Charlotte-Sophia of
  Mecklenburg-Strelitz, his wife.
The Princesses
  Charlotte Augusta ⎫
  Augusta   ⎬ daughters of
  Elizabeth   ⎪ King George
  Mary   ⎪ and
  Sophia   ⎪ Queen Charlotte.
  Amelia   ⎭
Lord Malmesbury, equerry to George,
  Prince of Wales.
Duke Frederick William of Würtemberg.
William, Duke of Gloucester.
Brigadier-General Brent Spencer.
George, Prince of Wales, Regent, later
  became George IV.
Princess Caroline of Brunswick, his
  wife.

Princess Charlotte, their daughter.

Mrs. Udney, governess to the Princess Charlotte.

Colonel Charles Fitzroy, husband of the Princess Amelia.

Miss Cornelia Knight, lady-companion to the Princess Charlotte.

William, Prince of Orange, betrothed to the Princess Charlotte.

Thomas FitzClarence, bastard son of William, Duke of Clarence.

Prince Leopold of Coburg, husband of the Princess Charlotte.

Sir Thomas Lawrence, portrait painter to the Prince of Wales.

Mrs. Griffiths, midwife.

Dr. Richard Croft, accoucheur.

Dr. Stockmar, physician to Prince Leopold.

Edward, Duke of Kent, father of Queen Victoria.

Madame de St. Laurent, his morganatic wife.

Victoria, Duchess of Kent, his legal wife.

William, Duke of Clarence, later
  became William IV.
Queen Adelaide, his wife.
Mrs. Maria Fitzherbert, morganatic
  wife of the Prince of Wales.

BUCKINGHAM PALACE

April 25, 1857

It was the old lady's eightieth birthday, an occasion, one might think, for rejoicing, although she upon whom this signal honour had fallen experienced little sense of pride or achievement, more an utter weariness brought on by the contemplation of her heavy burden of years. For over an hour she had been receiving her guests, accepting their false-hearty assurances that she would live to see many more birthdays, wondering whether they found it repellent to bow over and kiss her paper-skinned hand, that hand which she tried, in vain, to keep from trembling.

Lips, old and young, touched her fingers unceasingly; eyes, old and young, smiled into hers, seeking, questioning eyes, which yearned to discover the secrets of her heart. Some remembered her brother, that King of Pleasure, who had spent such prodigious sums of money for his own amusement; some remembered her sister, who had borne a child outside the bonds of matrimony; a few remembered her father, in the days before he had degenerated into a wraith-like figure haunting the lonely corridors of Windsor Castle and mumbling profanities; some remembered . . . all wondered. It made her want to laugh to hear them murmuring their polite felicitations, as though she were in some way to be commended for her own longevity; as though she merited a great deal of praise for staying alive for eight-and-a-half decades; as though she would willingly clothe her spirit in this obdurate, clinging flesh, these earthly shackles which so stubbornly refused to be shrugged off.

Each new day, after she had recovered

from her mild surprise at waking to see another dawn, she would silently command her legs to convey her from her bed to her commode without causing her pain. They would not. She would command her eyes to distinguish yellow silk from green as she bent to her tambourwork, but always the colours would merge into a blurred whole, and she would weep weak tears of frustration. In the long evenings her ears would strain to hear Vicky's singing, but the sweet, clear soprano constantly eluded her, and she was wont to fidget with irritation until the song was done. No, it was not praiseworthy to be old. It was not fortunate.

The rich fruit cake, with its layers of marzipan and pink icing, was giving her indigestion. Greedily she consumed it. Pleasure before pain. That was the way of life, the inexorable, unwritten law. Gently she belched behind her hand and glanced guiltily about her. Nobody had noticed. They were all conversing noisily, seemingly unmindful of her presence, grandly enthroned in Vicky's gold-damasked chair. The young were so selfish, so uncaring of the needs of the old. One day they too would know what it was to have stiff limbs, aching backs and failing sight. They too would experience the bitter pain of feeling unwanted, unloved, of knowing that they had outlived their time, of becoming an embarrassing, disturbing anachronism.

The old lady's gaze assessed her surroundings, resting briefly on the dining-table of gleaming red mahogany, which she instantly dismissed as a modern monstrosity; admiring the carved, shield-back chairs, upholstered in blue damask, which Mr. Hepplewhite had made for her mother; turning in horror from the Turkish ottoman, which she had seen displayed at Albert's Exhibition six years previously. There really wasn't much she did like about her brother George's palace. It had been designed for him by John Nash, upon the site of Buckingham House. The older building, erected in 1705 for the Duke of Buckingham, had been bought by her father, King George III, as a town house for Mama. It had been smaller then, not so draughty. Poor George, he could not build a family so he built palaces instead, in the hope that people would remember him for something other than his excesses.

There was Vicky, talking to Lord Palmerston, old 'Pam'. She was laughing, lifting her chin, parting her lips over very fine teeth. How successfully she concealed her dislike of her Prime Minister. Once she would not have been so circumspect. That spoiled young creature of eighteen, who had ascended the throne of England twenty years ago, would have coldly ignored that which did not please her. As she formulated this thought the old lady wondered whether she was being entirely fair to her niece. It was, after all, Vicky's mother, the Duchess of Kent — not here today, thank God — who had instilled into her daughter the idea that she could have anything in the world once the crown was placed upon her head, that other people did not matter, that duty was a word inconsistent with sovereignty, a word to be applied only to those who served the sovereign. Vicky had been so alone when she became Queen. Small wonder that she had clung, with something like desperation, to Lord Melbourne, that old charmer, with his ladies of ease discreetly tucked away in their little love-nests, clung to him with such youthful tenacity as to give rise to a scandal, and set abroad the rumour that the two were lovers. All nonsense, of course. Vicky, fatherless since the age of eight months, had needed a substitute-father, and Melbourne had filled the bill to perfection.

The old lady removed some cake crumbs from the corners of her mouth with a lace-trimmed handkerchief and met the glance of her niece's husband. Albert smiled and bowed politely, immediately resuming his conversation with the Prince of Wales. Judging by the expression on his handsome face one would almost think that he hated the boy. Unlike Vicky, the passage of time had not mellowed Albert. He was as cold, as uncompromising as ever. He still audited the household accounts with ruthless efficiency, still forced elderly duchesses, including herself! to stand on shaking legs for three hours at a stretch at the monthly drawing-rooms, still insisted on choosing Vicky's hats and gowns, and dear God, what execrable taste he displayed in both! To do Albert justice, he did have a keen sense of duty, though he had never thought it necessary, or indeed desirable, to woo his wife's subjects, and they, having set out to hate him with all the heartiness of which your average Englishman is capable, had ended up by despising him. They treated him with a kindly contempt which, had he deigned to notice its existence, would have added to the bitterness he felt at their gross ingratitude for his untiring efforts on their behalf. There was a great deal of good in Albert. If only he would let himself go occasionally, and prove to them all that he had *feelings*.

Shifting restlessly in her chair, the old lady smoothed her green velvet skirts with that recalcitrant, quivering hand. Vicky was bending over her, her clear blue eyes full of kindly concern. How pretty she looked in that pink figured silk with the lace ruffles. Who could believe that she had been delivered of her ninth child just ten days ago? The Queen of England deftly removed a slipping plate of Sèvres porcelain from her aunt's lap. 'More cake, dearest?'

Old, discerning eyes looked up at the Queen under a high brow crinkled into a frown of worry. Their owner said anxiously, 'The baby, my dear. Shall you call her Charlotte? Please?' The appeal ended on a high, querulous note of inquiry.

The Queen's smiling mouth straightened. She put on, as she herself would have phrased it, her 'firm' expression, the one she habitually used to control the whims of her children. 'No, dear,' she replied gently. 'She is to be called Beatrice Mary Victoria Feodore.' Quickly she elaborated, forestalling petulant objections, 'Beatrice, because I think it is such a pretty name; Mary, for you, my dear; Victoria, for her mother,' she dimpled charmingly, 'and Feodore, for my dear sister.'

A tear trickled down the aged, powdered cheek. 'Charlotte is a name so very precious to me,' she murmured fretfully. 'Mother was called so and dear George's girl. Unkind, so very unkind of you, Vicky . . .'

The Queen looked briefly over her shoulder to ascertain whether or not Albert had overheard the exchange, but he seemed totally absorbed in his conversation with Bertie. Why, she asked herself crossly, does Bertie always look so *nervous* when dearest Albert engages him in conversation? A hand plucked at her sleeve. The frail, reedy voice complained, '*One* of your daughters should have been named for Charlotte.'

The eyes of the Queen were drawn, as though by an invisible magnet, to a portrait which hung in the darkest corner of the Red Saloon, near the fireplace. Lawrence's portrait of the Princess Charlotte, painted only a few weeks prior to her death, seemed to leap out at her, reminding her sharply of the fickleness of fate, which had decreed Charlotte's death in child-bed, and had set in motion a train of events precursing her own advent into the world. She preferred not to dwell upon those events. They were at best undignified and at worst ludicrous, and ludicrous was not a word she could equably contemplate as bearing any relation to herself. The very name of Charlotte brought into immediate and painfully sharp focus the singular set of circumstances leading up to her birth. She detested the sound of it.

The portrait smiled at her, the eyes very like hers, the head set at that same lofty angle of arrogance so often reflected by her own mirror, the full lips bursting with embryo speech. The Queen said, with an assumption of sadness, 'Uncle George's daughter was so unfortunate, my dear. It is foolish of me, I know, but I should not care for one of my darlings to bear her name.'

A slight, wounding smile curved the old lady's pallid lips. 'How accomplished you are at self-delusion, Vicky.' She chuckled, with a degree of malice which shocked her niece, and went on in her cracked voice, 'You know very well that had Charlotte lived, you would not have seen the light of day. Your father, my brother, was already married, *à la main gauche*, to that actress woman who called herself Madame de St. Laurent. They had houses all over the world, you know, at Quebec, Gibraltar, and even here in London, right under Papa's nose. They . . . '

The Queen's face was transformed. It bore a withered, stricken look, and bright spots of colour flagged her

11

cheeks. She begged God to make her aunt stop giving tongue to these terrible reminiscences. When she spoke her voice shook. 'I . . . I sh . . . shall get you some more cake, my dear.'

'It gives me indigestion,' came the grumbling, graceless reply. The old lady watched the small, graceful figure move towards the huge dining-table, with its gallant array of delectable foods prepared in her honour. With the capriciousness of the very elderly she swung between compassion for and condemnation of, the woman who now sat upon the throne once occupied by her father and two of her brothers. It was good for Vicky to be reminded of those things she tried so hard to forget. People no longer believed in the divinity of kings.

The Princess Royal, correct and dutiful, came to sit beside her great-aunt. 'Pussy' they called her. What a ridiculously childish name for one who was shortly to be married. Pussy smiled brightly. 'Dearest Aunt, permit me to say that you are looking very well. I hope you are enjoying your birthday party?'

But the old lady would not respond to the naïve, well-meant pleasantries. The desire to inflict hurt upon those she loved bubbled away inside her, lingering, demanding assuagement.

'I do not like that person you are to marry, child,' she said severely. 'He is cold, like your father.'

Pussy was so surprised to hear this criticism of her kind, beloved Papa, whom she thought the most wonderful person in the whole world, that her mind refused to register the slight to her betrothed. She could only stare at her great-aunt and wonder whether encroaching senility could be the cause of such an outrageous suggestion. With a nice sense of diplomacy which, in other circumstances, would have done credit to her mother, Pussy side-stepped neatly, 'Dearest Aunt, may I get you some more cake?'

Alas, she could not have chosen a

more unfortunate remark. The old lady's pent-up antagonism exploded into unbridled wrath. She struggled to her feet, groping for her malacca cane, 'Cake! Cake! Why do you all insist that I shall eat more cake? It gives me wind in my belly!' She was shouting, drawing every eye in the room towards her, momentarily transfixing her guests into horrified immobility. 'I do not like him!' she stormed at the scarlet-cheeked Pussy, who instantly dissolved into tears and ran into the sheltering arms of her Papa. The old lady ignored Pussy's distress and the host of curious, staring eyes directed towards her, and ranted on. 'He murdered his first wife, you know. Murdered her in cold blood. Würtemberg. What is that? A puppet-kingdom ruled over by Napoleon Bonaparte. I . . . ' Strong arms encircled her waist. She stared up into the stern, troubled face of Prince Albert. 'Leopold,' she murmured. 'She is dead. Charlotte is dead, Leopold.'

'Yes, dear,' he soothed. 'Let me take you to bed.'

Her hands clawed at his immaculately arranged stock. 'Royal will not stop crying. Tell her to stop, Leopold, because Mama does not like it. She thinks it will make Papa ill again . . . '

Part One

THE HAREM

KEW

1796

Royal's unrestrained sobbing could be heard as far away as Mr. Chambers' Gothic pavilion, where her younger sisters sat stitching away at linen chemises destined for the Hostel for Destitute and Fallen Girls at Islington. The constant pricking of fingers embellished the coarse material with tiny red spots, prompting the sisters to dub their hated, never-ending task the 'piebald pop-overs', an expression which Mama deprecated and Papa found vastly amusing. A varied assortment of insect life inhabited the darkest corners of the Pavilion, and the royal ladies sat with their feet propped on wooden footstools, in order to avoid the unpleasant explorations of wild life over their feet and ankles.

The Princess Amelia, near to tears herself at the frightful calamity which had befallen Royal, threw aside her work with an air of hysterical abandon and sprang to her feet. Having come to an important decision she announced it to the other four: 'I am going in to comfort her.' Her rosy face expressed a mixture of apprehension and defiance.

Augusta, whose long Guelph nose dominated a face which might otherwise have been considered handsome, protested loudly against this act of rebellion. 'Mama said that Lottie was to be left alone until she has regained command of herself,' she reminded her youngest sister. 'You will remain here, Amelia.' In the absence of Royal, temporarily *hors de combat*, Augusta, who was next in order of seniority, took over the role of guide and mentor to her younger sisters, a role not always acknowledged and rarely appreciated by the others.

Mary and Sophia, though not indifferent to Royal's sufferings, stood too much in awe of Mama to disobey her, but Elizabeth, with a shocking display of crooked teeth, yawned widely, sucked her sore fingers and rising to her feet, declared truculently, 'Well, I for one am going in. I have had quite enough of goodly works for today, my dears. The Destitute Girls may run about naked as far as I am concerned. I shall not stitch another piebald pop-over for the rest of this week.' She gave an exaggerated shiver. 'Besides, it is growing cold out here, and even Mama cannot expect us to nest in the open like the birds until Royal has *regained command of herself*.' The last words were pronounced in mocking imitation of Augusta's flat, pedantic tones.

Mary, fair and delicate of feature, undoubtedly the best-looking of the royal sisters, giggled at Lizzie's 'take-off'. 'It must be after six o'clock,' she guessed. With a brief, surreptitious glance at her watch, Augusta, sensing herself to be on the brink of defeat and wisely withdrawing her guns, countered firmly, 'As it is almost time for supper we shall go in, but we shall *not* go into the drawing-room.'

'*I* shall go where I please, Gussie.' Elizabeth tossed her curls at her sister, and quitting the pavilion before Augusta could draw breath to argue, ran across the lawn, her sprigged muslin skirts bunched indecorously high above her ankles. Augusta, forsaken and annihilated, ran after her wayward sister, while the other three, glad of an opportunity to relinquish their odious work, followed in hot pursuit.

The five girls, gay as butterflies in their flowered silks and muslins, darted across the smoothly sloping lawns and entered the house by the garden door. Heedless of Augusta's breathless protests, Elizabeth sped down the passage leading to the Queen's drawing-room, from whence the sound of weeping still issued, though weakened now by lack of attention and sheer physical exhaustion.

Charlotte Augusta Matilda, Princess Royal of England, plain 'Royal' to her sisters, presented a pitiable sight. She lay sprawled across the middle section of a confidante settee, her ample proportions encased in unseasonable green velvet trimmed with black lace — a personal tribute to her ruined hopes — and dabbed ineffectually at her swollen eyelids with a wet wisp of cambric and lace. Blonde curls clung damply to her plump, flushed cheeks and her lower lip trembled uncontrollably. Unkind comparison might have likened her face to a pink blancmange, which had that very moment been turned out on to a plate, and waited, in shivering anticipation, for the assault of the spoon.

The sight of her sisters, crowding curiously into the drawing-room, occasioned a fresh outburst of weeping. 'He is my last chance!' she wailed dramatically. 'I am thirty-one!' This cryptic statement was greeted by uniformly sympathetic murmurings from her sisters who knew that Papa would be equally reluctant to lose any one of them should some predatory male dare to cast covetous eyes in their direction.

'The Duke of Würtemberg is very fat, Lottie,' ventured Sophia the peacemaker, the pourer of oil on troubled waters. 'Lord Malmesbury says he eats a whole capon at a single sitting!'

Royal sat up and blew her nose, a loud, violent trumpeting. 'He *offered* for me,' she returned sullenly, 'and Papa accepted, and I would have had some *status* at last, a household of my own and servants to do *my* bidding. I do not care if he is a yard wide and has two heads. He is a man, and I need a man!'

This astounding revelation reduced Royal's sisters to bemused silence, but with the exception of Amelia, who was just thirteen, they were only too well aware of Royal's predicament. Secret, furtive explorations of their bodies, after the candles were out, had revealed strange, unsatisfied longings which they had correctly surmised could only be relieved by the touch of a man. They had tall, lusty brothers who fondled them frequently, teasing, unwittingly arousing. They knew and they did not know. They yearned and burned and wondered why headaches and fainting spells were so much a feature of their lives.

Royal's inflamed eyes filled again. 'And now Papa says there is a reason why I may not marry the Duke, but he will not tell me what that reason is. *He will not tell me!*' She clenched her fists in her lap and ground her teeth together, fighting back a scream, an indulgence which Mama, presently taking the air with her ladies, would never forgive. 'Oh, it is so unfair,' she moaned, hugging herself and rocking back and forth. 'Our brothers may marry where they please, low-born women like Maria Fitzherbert and Dorothy Jordan.'

Augusta snorted a contemptuous rebuttal of this statement. 'George is married to Caroline of Brunswick and Maria Fitzherbert is now relegated to the status of mistress, which indeed she always was, despite that fancy little ceremony at Park Street, and which she always will be.'

'Poor Caroline,' commiserated Mary. 'She must find it very lonely living at Blackheath. I think George was very cruel to cast her off like that, only a month after she had borne him a daughter.'

'Nine months to the very day,' put in Amelia precociously and stifled a giggle as Augusta frowned at her. Royal sniffed her disdain. 'He only married her to please Papa, and to get his debts paid for him. Papa made it a condition that he would settle George's debts if he agreed to marry. When I asked George if he thought he would like Caroline he said, 'One damned frau is as good as another'.'

Amelia chewed her finger-nail. 'I wonder why George does not like her though? She is quite pretty and has an agreeable nature, you know.'

Augusta wrinkled her nose, sat down at the harpsichord and thumped out a

26

few chords. 'She smells because she does not wash, and she does not change her under-linen more than once a month. Lady Jersey told me.'

'George is very fastidious,' agreed Amelia primly.

'Lady Jersey would say that,' sniffed Mary. 'She would very much like to bear the title of Princess of Wales herself.'

'Moreover,' pursued Augusta, with a rebuking glance at her sisters for interrupting the catalogue of Caroline's failings, 'she has a very loud, coarse voice.'

'Do you think that George will go back to Mrs. Fitzherbert now?' asked Sophia. The question was directed at Augusta, who shrugged carelessly. 'Who knows what George will do? He has Lady Jersey to comfort him these days. Caroline was right when she remarked that the only *faux pas* she ever committed was in marrying the husband of Mrs. Fitzherbert.'

The others trilled with laughter, vying with one another in recalling anecdotes of Caroline's all too numerous blunders.

'What about the time she told Lady Jersey that she did not in the least mind George having a mistress?'

'Yes, and that day we all dined at Carlton House and she blew a kiss at Papa!'

'Do you suppose that she and Lord Canning are lovers?' It was Augusta who put an end to these extravagances. 'Caroline is a foolish woman,' she declared with severity. 'She lets her tongue run away with her.'

Amelia asked curiously, 'Have you ever seen Mrs. Fitzherbert, Gussie?'

Augusta looked shocked. 'Heavens, no. Mama would never permit us to see a woman like that. She is a whore and what is worse, she is a Catholic!'

'One would have thought,' remarked Sophia 'that George would have got himself a son before deserting Caroline. Queens Regnant have never been popular in England.'

'It is strange, is it not, to think that little Charlotte will one day be Queen of

England in her own right?' mused Mary.

Augusta slammed down the lid of the harpsichord and commented shrewdly, 'If George does not take it into his head to divorce Caroline and marry again.'

Mary shook her head doubtfully. 'Papa would not like that.' There were murmurs of agreement.

Royal, alarmed by the fact that attention seemed to be slipping away from her and her troubles, applied her handkerchief to her eyes again and lamented, 'Papa is so cruel. I had a very good chance to marry one of the Bourbon princes eight years ago, but he was most uncivil to the French ambassador, Papa I mean, and sent him from Windsor without even offering him accommodation for the night.'

Elizabeth, who with her customary zeal for food — a zeal which had earned her the nickname of 'Fatima' — was delving with gusto into a bowl of white grapes, her plump bottom wedged into one of the small Barjier chairs attached to each end of the settee, interposed idly, 'Papa was ill then. Not himself, my dears. Before Mama sent us to Weymouth I saw him put his hand down the front of Lady Pembroke's gown. He had her trapped fast against the wall — ' Elizabeth bubbled with merriment, — 'and she kept trying to curtsey, which made Papa's hand jump about like a jack-in-the-box!'

Elizabeth extricated some pips from between her two front teeth and popped four more grapes into her mouth. Her speech became muffled. 'And then there was the time . . . mm . . . when he set fire to . . . mmmm . . . Mama's bed-curtains with the flame from a candle . . . and . . . mm, took George by the throat . . . ' She prattled on, chewing happily on the grapes, unaware that she had said anything at all remarkable which could account for the odd looks of frozen horror on the faces of her sisters. Interpreting Augusta's fixed, glassy stare as an expression of her disbelief she challenged, 'If you do not believe me,

Gussie, ask Lady Harcourt. She was there.'

'Elizabeth!' The high, fluting voice, coming from the direction of the doorway, caused Elizabeth to swing round sharply to face her mother. Queen Charlotte, dressed in an outdated green silk gown in the polonaise style, diminutive in stature, formidable of mien, glided into the drawing-room. She regarded her talkative daughter coolly, giving no sign that she had overheard her indiscretions, and said reprovingly, 'I thought, Elizabeth, that you had given me a promise to sketch the view from my bedroom window, after you had completed your allotted quota of stitching. Why are you not doing so, my dear?'

Elizabeth, relieved to be let off so lightly, essayed a precarious curtsey, almost overbalanced with nervousness, recovered and ran. The Queen's wide mouth compressed into a line of pained disapproval. 'How I dislike, my dears, to find you idle,' she rebuked. 'God

31

expects the time He has given us on earth to be profitably employed.'

Red with embarrassment the girls rose from their curtseys, praying for instant dismissal. Charlotte surveyed her brood of daughters, five out of the fifteen children she had borne during the first twenty years of her marriage, thirteen of whom still survived. What a problem they were, these marriageable girls, with their greensick fancies, their vapours and their gossipy ways. She had indeed found it too mortifying to rebuke Elizabeth for her flippant remarks, which had cut like a knife into her heart, too painful to remember her husband's 'eccentricities', which, please God, would never be repeated.

She caught sight of herself in the long pier glass fixed to the wall, next to Zoffany's portrait of her. The image in oils and the reality in flesh and bone did not resemble each other. The coloured, two-dimensional representation of a woman flattered. The drab, three-dimensional, solid reality was . . . reality.

She thought: I am ugly. Not merely plain but downright ugly. *Hässlich*. And green does not suit me, and my wig needs recurling, and even if I change my gown and my wig I shall still be ugly, because my eyes are too big and my mouth is too wide and my nose is too flat. Perhaps my fecundity redeems my lack of looks? Inwardly she laughed at her own self-denigration, or was it inverted self-pity? Fifteen children, and what a liability they were proving. There was George, her eldest, her darling, with his ever-changing mistresses, his morganatic marriage and his dotty, discarded wife; Frederick, with as many mistresses, his poorly-dowered, eccentric little German wife, his legal wife, his barren wife; William, and Mrs. Dorothy Jordan, an actress, who had the bad taste to produce a bastard a year — a bevy of FitzClarences; and Edward with his pert little actress who called herself Madame de St. Laurent, and who was really Thérèse de Mongenet, or even plain Julie Sinclair. And one must not forget Augustus, who had married the Lady Augusta Murray. Fortunately Augustus had been young enough for the King to extricate him forcibly from that unsuitable entanglement, and the marriage had been annulled.

Charlotte continued to stare at her reflection. How was it possible for an ugly little woman like herself to produce such handsome male progeny? After a minute or two of this silent self-appraisal her eyes, enormous brown orbs, flickered back to her daughters. The sight of Royal's woebegone face brought her sharply back to the present and to contemplation of the problem yet to be resolved — whether or not her eldest daughter should be allowed to marry the Duke of Würtemberg. The King had said she might, until he was informed by one of his ambassadors that there was a rumour abroad to the effect that the Duke had murdered his first wife, Caroline of Brunswick's sister. Lord Malmesbury, he who had brought Caroline of Brunswick to England to marry the Prince of Wales, he of the discreet, diplomatic tongue, had been despatched to the tiny German state of Würtemberg to sift the truth of the matter. Only that morning had come word that Malmesbury was back in England and making for Kew. Soon Royal's fate would be decided. Charlotte hoped sincerely that rumour lied. Royal, with her fits of hysteria and her constant grumbling about lack of status, was becoming a nuisance.

It was unfortunate, reflected Charlotte, that the King had this stubborn reluctance to permit his daughters to marry. It was not quite normal really. Charlotte hastily pushed this thought aside. George, her husband, was perfectly normal. She repeated these words to herself several times, like an incantation. Eight years ago he had had a mysterious and unfortunate malady which had defied diagnosis. It would not happen again. Please God, it would not happen again. At the time, George had been terribly worried about the loss of the American colonies, and then there had been that business of the woman, Mary Robinson, another actress, threatening to publish certain letters she had received from the Prince of Wales, a threat which had cost the King three thousand pounds to conquer. Almost simultaneously with the affair of the Robinson woman the King's brother, the Duke of Cumberland, had married a commoner, in despite of the Royal Marriage Act of 1772, which expressly forbade any member of the Royal family to do so without the permission of the King. Yes, it had been a very trying time. Small wonder that George had become ill. Pray God that Malmesbury brought good news.

Charlotte pulled her ragged thoughts into a semblance of order. First things first. 'My dears,' she said brightly, 'there is time before supper to practice your music.' She clapped her hands together, an unfortunate habit left over from her children's nursery days. 'Go, go along

now. Herr Bach awaits you in the Music
Room.'

★   ★   ★

'Well, Lord Malmesbury, and what is it
to be? Marriage, or perpetual virginity
for my eldest daughter?' her flippant
tone, uncharacteristic, even shocking in
one so unfailingly correct, was belied by
the fluttering hands and the slight,
almost imperceptible tremor of her
chin. He noticed and was surprised by
her lack of composure. He struggled to
formulate a diplomatic reply, but before
he had time to assemble his thoughts,
she said, 'It was so good of you, Lord
Malmesbury, to come to me before
going to the King at Windsor. It shall be
our secret, yes?'

He smiled and bowed an acknowledgement of the coquettish sentiment
delivered, however, without the least
touch of coyness. 'Our secret, Madam,'
he assured her.

She laughed, a peculiarly cracked

sound, which issued from the wide, reptilian mouth in short, sharp bursts of sound. Very large teeth were exposed to view. 'Does Lady Malmesbury keep secrets from you, Malmesbury?'

'Ma'am, I have not the least doubt of it,' came the grave rejoinder, 'especially when such secrets concern the entirely unnecessary purchase of an expensive satin bonnet.'

Her smile grew wider, then quickly dissolved, gentle raillery replaced by the desire to explain, to excuse her unprecedented conduct, for never, in thirty-five years of marriage, had she ever practised a deceit upon her husband. She began diffidently. 'It is difficult for me, you understand, Malmesbury. I am most anxious for my eldest daughter to be settled in life. Poor child, she is always so concerned about her lack of status, as she puts it. Her temperament is not at all suited to the maiden state, and she is singularly lacking in the accomplishments which might make life bearable for her were she to remain unmarried. Music is anathema to her. She is unable to recognize a true note when she hears one. She does not like riding, and she can sleep through an entire opera.' The brown eyes twinkled. 'Though anyone who can doze through Herr Mozart's 'Nozze di Figaro' displays a talent of sorts, I suppose.'

He smiled his appreciation of this quip, while she continued in more serious vein, 'I am, alas, unable to persuade His Majesty of the truth of this. He is most unwilling to part with our daughters. He is afraid that they will not receive at the hands of their husbands the kindness and understanding they have always enjoyed from a loving father.'

He made comforting, comprehending noises and wondered why this anxious little woman was so disliked by those who served her. She had ever been a kind, thoughtful mistress, and but a moment since had displayed her impish sense of humour. The reason, he supposed, was not far to seek. From the moment she had set foot in England, not a month, in fact, after the ceremonials attendant on her wedding and Coronation had been completed, she had been promptly banished to the realms of domesticity by a dictatorial, pompous young man of three and twenty who regarded her without love, but as a convenient, if undecorative, vehicle for producing children. The burgeoning, lively intellect of the young Charlotte Sophia of Mecklenburg-Strelitz had been buried forever beneath a mass of nursery trivia, occasioned by her unending pregnancies. Her opinion was consulted on nothing more remarkable than the proper remedy for croup, the precise age for infant weaning, or the advantages for and against of Dr. Jenner's new system of innoculation against the smallpox. The Queen of England was little more than a German hausfrau, burdened with the additional responsibility of having to appear in public three or four times a year, when, decked out in her finery, she must endeavour to play the Queen in fact as well as in name. Outwardly, apart from a regrettable tendency to adopt the role of petty tyrant with the members of her own household, she had remained complacent and uncomplaining, never raising her voice, save perhaps to reprimand her boisterous children. Now that she had at last lifted a hand to fight for her daughter's happiness, she was suffering vague twinges of conscience because she had 'deceived' the King.

With a guilty start Lord Malmesbury realized that he had committed the deadly sin of staring at royalty. She, for her part, was regarding him with a certain quizzical amusement. 'Have I a smut upon my nose, Malmesbury?'

He pulled himself together, apologizing profusely for his lapse, his round, red face comically dismayed. 'I was musing upon the fact that Your Majesty will have been married for thirty-five years next month,' he improvised skilfully, and not altogether untruth-fully.

'By the look on your face you were thinking about a great deal more besides,' she observed, laughing at his confusion. To dispel his embarrassment she went on briskly, 'Come now, tell me the news from Würtemberg.' She clasped her hands together tightly, like a little girl about to embark upon the recitation of a difficult poem. 'Oh, I do so hope that it is favourable.' His lowered gaze warned her and her large mouth drooped. 'It is not good?'

Lord Malmesbury's clenched hand covered a small, prefatory cough. He hated to disappoint her, but the truth must be told. 'It is not so bad as His Majesty feared,' he began cautiously, feeling his way, wanting to please, yet too honest to attempt deception. 'It appears that the Duke was very inebriated on the night that his wife was taken ill. Thinking her also to be the victim of over-indulgence, he neglected to call her physician when she complained of a pain in her chest. Imprudently he dosed her with rum and then took to his bed. Two hours later she died, while he was still sleeping off the results of his tippling.' He paused delicately, mentally phrasing his summing-up in the most tactful manner possible. 'Ma'am,' he concluded, 'the Duke of Würtemberg is not guilty of wilful murder, but he *is* guilty of brutal neglect, and I would not therefore recommend him as a suitable husband for your beloved daughter.'

For a very long time she said nothing. The narrowed eyes and screwed-up mouth gave him the impression that she was about to weep. He looked down at his feet. The silence lengthened intolerably, until he felt that every muscle in his body was taut as a fiddle-string. When she spoke at last he almost burst with relief as he listened to her perfectly-controlled, measured pronouncement, which, though biting, was infinitely preferable to that agonizing nothingness. 'I did not intend, Malmesbury, that your coming here should be for the purpose of giving me an opinion upon the character of the Duke of Würtemberg. As to that, His Majesty will be the judge. His Majesty was anxious that you should ascertain the true facts surrounding the death of the Duchess of Würtemberg. That is all. You have performed your commission to our complete satisfaction and for that we are very grateful.' Her last words, spoken with a stiff little smile, nullified the stinging reprimand. He mumbled an apology for his presumption, but she waved it aside and gave him permission to withdraw. As he reached the door she called after him, 'Lord Malmesbury!' He turned, directing at her a look of polite inquiry. Her smile was self-condemning. 'Thanks, good friend.'

He bowed, acknowledging the implied compliment, touched by the look of near-despair on her plain face. He recalled that once before he had neglected to give an opinion — even when pressed to do so — over the matter of the Prince of Wales's intended bride, whom he knew to be altogether unsuitable. Well, he had given it this time, and if another royal marriage ended in disaster it would not be on his conscience. Quietly, Lord Malmesbury closed the door behind him.

Left alone, Charlotte paced the length of the drawing-room, taking short, rapid strides, seizing this rare moment of complete privacy to make her decision. Her daughter was thirty-one, still young enough to bear a child. A child would be a comfort to Lottie if her husband should prove less than satisfactory, or if, as might be expected, she suffered early widowhood. Lottie was a strong girl. It was not unlikely that Würtemberg would predecease her, especially having regard to his mode of life, which, it must be admitted, resembled to a large degree that of the Prince of Wales. Charlotte did not dwell for long upon this unwelcome reflection. In the event of her daughter becoming a widow, she would live on in Würtemberg for the remainder of her days, her status, which she prized so highly, firmly established. The Queen nodded to herself, picked up a silver bell, and rang for her ladies.

1797

The Red Saloon at Kew Palace was filled to bursting with a noisy crowd of wedding guests, who chattered, flirted, placed bets on the date, and even on the hour of birth of the first fruit of the union which they had come to witness, and generally behaved themselves with less circumspection than a class of rowdy school children — one could not lay the birch to those plump, regal, foreign posteriors and bid *them* be quiet.

From the direction of the alcove issued the sound of weeping, plainly and embarrassingly audible. The King of England, red of face, protuberant of eye, with his handkerchief pressed firmly to his streaming eyes, slumped in his chair and watched his daughter being wrenched from his bosom by the fifty-year-old Duke Frederick William of Würtemberg. God-damned fellow was only nine years younger than himself. George undid two of the gold buttons securing his crimson and silver striped waistcoat and adjusted his Garter ribbon to cover the gap. All that steaming emotion inside him required an outlet. Metaphorically speaking, he could feel the evil humours pouring forth in an unending stream through that gap in his waistcoat. Never, never again would he let one of his darlings go. It was all too painful.

The Queen, on the other hand, sat straight-backed, dry-eyed and relieved, beside her husband, and thanked God for her eldest daughter's deliverance, a deliverance which had cost her mother a great deal more effort than the day she had pushed Charlotte Augusta into the world.

The bride, large and splendid in

white satin and Brussels lace, her elaborately curled golden head adorned with a circlet of diamonds sporting three osprey feathers, declaimed the responses with fearful clarity, engendering infectious smiles and causing laughing, whispered comments to run from mouth to mouth among the assembled ladies and gentlemen. Duke Frederick, who was six feet tall, with a disproportionate waist measurement of seventy-six inches — he really was a yard wide! — was undergoing some mental and physical stress resultant on an entire night spent in the company of the Prince of Wales, the dukes of York and Sussex, and the Duke of Clarence, the latter having torn himself from the arms of Mrs. Jordan in order to be present at the festivities. These gentlemen, having declared themselves honour-bound to 'see Würtemberg off,' had proceeded to do so by providing him with a whole barrel of Madeira and two actresses from Drury Lane all to himself, which stimulants had reduced him, figuratively speaking, to a mere shadow of his former self. The consequence was that he was having some difficulty in concentrating on the solemn words of the Marriage Service, despite the fact that the Archbishop of Canterbury, worldly-wise in the ways of royalty, was enunciating each word with more than his usual clarity of diction.

The Duke made his responses in muffled tones, yet loud enough to provoke more smiles as he croaked, 'Vith my body I thee vashup.' Fortunately for the bridegroom's peace of mind, he had his back to the guests and was therefore quite unable to see certain ill-concealed demonstrations of mirth taking place at his expense. He was, however, well aware that he had become something of a figure of fun to these English, who seemed to lose their sense of fitness when confronted by a foreigner, they being of the opinion that anything un-English was occasion for unbridled levity. The Duke's equerry had, rather tactlessly, shown him a cartoon, drawn by a man called Gillray, and representing in some detail an imagined consummation between a bride and her bridegroom. The cartoon was entitled 'Le Baiser à la Würtemberg'. Frederick William's first instinct had been to laugh, until his slow intellect took in the fact that the improbably fat figure sprawled on the Gargantuan bed, clad in a smocked night-shirt, was a crude caricature of himself, and that the pigeon-breasted, fat-legged creature beside him was meant to be the Princess Royal of England. No, the Duke did not particularly admire his bride's relatives, or his bride's father's subjects. He would be glad enough to whisk her off to Würtemberg.

Archbishop Moore pronounced the pair man and wife, delivered the blessing, gave the signal for the singing of the anthem, and indicated that the bridegroom might salute his bride. He did, very loudly and with a burst of enthusiasm brought on by relief that the

50

ceremony was over.

The sobbing in the alcove reached a wailing crescendo. This had the effect of unmanning the Prince of Wales, resplendent in a crimson velvet frock-coat frogged with gold, his fair hair curled and pomaded, who left the Saloon in a flurry of tears, closely followed by his brother York. The latter, being made of sterner stuff, sensed the need for immediate liquid refreshment.

Meanwhile, the Princess Augusta, to whom sentimentality was a sign of weakness, looked at Royal's radiant face and experienced a sharp pang of pure envy. Not that one could exactly term Royal's husband a 'catch', with his bladder-of-lard face, and his brown button eyes, embedded in folds of sagging flesh. Nevertheless she, Augusta, was only two years younger than her elder sister, with no sign of a prospective bridegroom waiting for her in Germany, or anywhere else for that matter. What did the future hold for her? Endless days of stitching piebald pop-overs? Music lessons with Herr Bach? Distributing Bibles to the poor? It was a dismal prospect.

Augusta's eye, which could bear no longer to look upon Royal's happiness, lighted on the tall figure of a military gentleman standing on the 'bride's side' of the Saloon. He turned his head and she saw that it was Brigadier-General Brent Spencer, a friend of her brother George. The Brigadier, as though cognisant of her regard, turned his head even further and looked directly at her. Without the least sign of embarrassment he smiled broadly and she, to her astonishment — for she was generally very correct in her demeanour towards her inferiors — found herself returning the smile. He was not a handsome man, she decided, rather too thin for her taste and with a nose like a bird of prey. His eyes, light brown in colour, extraordinarily brilliant and set rather close together, caused the 'hawk' simile to persist in her mind, though she hastily changed this to 'eagle'. Yes, Brigadier-General Brent Spencer looked like an eagle. Augusta had often passed the time of day with him, exchanging the usual banal pleasantries expected of her, but she had never before thought of him as a man, rather as an adjunct to the royal household, impersonal, functional, an obeyer of commands. Was it the gay wedding atmosphere which was making her think of nakedness and beds and delicious forbidden caresses? She felt the beginnings of a blush and tore her eyes away from that penetrating gaze. When she ventured to look again, certain that only the back of his head would be presented to her, her cheeks flamed into scarlet. He was laughing at her!

★   ★   ★

Elizabeth too was studying her eldest sister. Royal actually looked mighty handsome today. The white satin did make her full figure rather more apparent than usual, but then excess weight was a family problem. Elizabeth was only too well aware of her own thickening figure. She consoled herself with the thought that men preferred fat women. She had heard her brother Fred say so many times. Musings upon surplus flesh led naturally on towards musings upon the dainties waiting to tempt her receptive palate in the dining-saloon. Elizabeth's saliva glands began to work as she took her place in the procession already forming to go out of the Red Saloon. Royal was settled. It would be Gussie's turn next, then hers. She formed a mental picture of herself progressing down the Saloon on the arm of a handsome, slender, faceless German prince.

* * *

Mary, on the arm of her cousin, Prince William of Gloucester, looked up into his pale, vapid face and smiled. He grinned sheepishly down at her then looked quickly away. She thought him vastly unattractive, with his receding chin and his pimples. He was only a year younger than herself and yet she fancied him a child by comparison. She had tried to engage him in conversation during the ceremony, but he had remained stiff and gauche as a schoolboy and she had abandoned the effort in disgust. He was, after all, part commoner, which might explain his lack of elegance and sophistication. It was really rather shocking of Uncle Gloucester to have married the daughter of a woman who drove a rag-and-bone cart in Holborn, and foist upon the Royal family a half-and-half like Silly Billy. Mary dismissed her cousin as not worth her attention and concentrated her gaze upon bobbing head of Prince Frederi Brunswick, a few feet in front He had come over in the tra Duke of Würtemberg and h at her quite often. Papa not object to her marrying a prince of the house of Brunswick.

★   ★   ★

Sophia, walking behind Mary, looked about her for 'him'. A tingling sensation at the back of her neck, part imagination, part aching desire, had communicated to her the idea that he must be seated not far behind her, but she had not dared to turn round lest she betray her guilty secret to the all-seeing eye of Mama. She had known him for six months. Young and in love, the two were convinced that happiness would ultimately crown their efforts to be together, and that a marriage would be the King. As Sophia remarked, 'Royal is settled. how happy she is and marry in due st Sophie, am a reminded her. 'Papa dukedom,' she ng, and he, loving

her so much, believed the incredible
and hugged her to his heart. Sophia
craned her neck. She could not see him.
Perhaps later . . .

★ ★ ★

Amelia, uncomfortable in her first pair
of whalebone stays, which greatly
detracted from the joy of wearing a new
Greek-style gown embroidered with
gold thread, looked forward only to
being released from these tiresome
ceremonials and festivities so that she
might ride her mare in the park.

★ ★ ★

'I make you enceinte in one go, eh
liebchen?' Frederick William, wearing a
voluminous gown of white cambric,
incongruously embroidered with tiny
true-lovers' knots, a satin night-cap
adorning his balding head, heaved his
huge bulk into the marital bed and
made a grab for his palpitating bride.

She, nothing loath, popped a candied plum into her mouth, called him a 'great boaster', and submitted eagerly to his caresses. It was, she discovered, rather like having an elephant on top of one, but apart from this slight inconvenience, nothing could have been more diverting. The consummation was completed in very short order and with the briefest of struggles, where-upon the satiated bridegroom rolled off his bride, puffing like a porpoise, and was soon snoring with a degree of intensity which ensured Royal's continued wakefulness. She lay back, savouring her triumph, feeling vastly superior to her five sisters, who, poor creatures, had not yet been initiated and made privy to the 'great secret'. Happily for her, Royal was unaware that she had been cheated, and that there was a good deal more to love-making than the rapid in-and-out operation to which she had been subjected. All she knew was that dear Würtemberg had made her into a woman at last. In his small principality, a palace awaited the arrival of its new mistress, a host of servants waited to obey her lightest command, horses and carriages of her own waited to convey her hither and yon. She would send for some of that new japanned furniture advertised in the Third Edition of Mr. Hepplewhite's 'Cabinet Maker and Upholsterer's Guide'. Perhaps too she could persuade Herr Zoffany to come to Würtemberg and paint her portrait, holding her first child. Royal was convinced that she would be fruitful like Mama, even though Mama had had ten children by the time she was thirty-one.

'I make you enceinte in one go, eh liebchen?' The Duke of Würtemberg yawned prodigiously and reached for her. The Duchess of Würtemberg blew out the candle and fumbled for the box of comfits.

THE ROAD TO
WEYMOUTH

1800

The rough jolting of the badly-sprung
coach made Sophia feel miserably
uncomfortable, a disease of body not
unmixed with anger that Mama had not
seen fit to provide her with the latest
addition to the royal mews, a neat little
carriage upholstered in red leather,
ornamented with silver joints and
lamps, and fitted with the new whip
springs, this last a refinement which
added considerably to the comfort of
the passengers. The baby was positively
leaping about inside her, adding to her
distress by inducing a feeling of
incipient nausea.

Sophia's niece, the four-year-old
Princess Charlotte, fidgeted about on
the lap of her governess, Mrs. Udney,

exclaiming at every strange and enchanting sight to be glimpsed from the mud-spattered windows of the coach, and generally contributing to the minor hazards of the journey by thrusting her bright yellow head out of the window from time to time, in order to shriek her unsolicited opinions to some passing sheep-herd or plodding wayfarer. These frequent breaches of discipline were frowned upon by the distracted governess, who was finding it a very different kettle of fish to control her wriggling charge within the confines of a swaying coach. Mrs. Udney longed for the stability and serenity of the nursery at Carlton House, where infringements of discipline could be firmly punished by a slap on the bottom and fifteen minutes on the 'quiet' stool.

The Princess Mary, a copy of Fanny Burney's 'Evelina' propped on her lap, dozed fitfully in an effort to escape from the general pandemonium surrounding her. Sophia envied Mary her detachment, envied and resented, because her elder sister showed so little concern for her condition. To look at Mary one would imagine the bearing of a bastard to be an everyday occurrence. Mary is very level-headed thought Sophia. Doubtless she is of the opinion that I am a fool for allowing my animal instincts to get the better of me. What a trap had her body become. What a price must she pay for one night of furtive joy in the gardens of Kew, a desperate, painful coupling among the beetles and spiders which inhabited the lower regions of the Chinese pagoda, with fear her constant companion; fear of discovery; fear that he would despise her for her forwardness; and afterwards fear of the consequences. Tears, which came readily to Sophia these days, welled up and trickled down her cheeks. She brushed them away with her gloved hand, casting a guilty glance at the flushed face of Mrs. Udney. For once Sophia blessed Charlotte's naughtiness. The harassed governess had little thought to spare for anything other than the restraining of the difficult, high-spirited child.

★   ★   ★

Three years had passed since the Princess Sophia had fallen in love with her commoner. Three long years of raised hopes, followed by crushing disappointments, for after Royal's departure it had gradually become apparent that Papa did not intend to give any more of his darlings away. He had said as much, bemoaning the fact that he had let his dear Lottie fall into the hands of that 'fat pig from Würtemberg'. 'One stillborn child he gave her!' Papa had shouted, waving his arms in the air. 'What good is that for my cherished one, hey? Hey? Tell me, what good is that?' and receiving no answer from his glum wife and daughters, 'He does not love her. No, no, he does not. He does not make her happy.' The staccato tirade had flowed on until Sophia thought she would burst asunder with frustration, but one never presumed to argue with Papa. As usual the princesses suppressed their emotions and laid yet a further strain upon their twanging nerves.

Offers of marriage for the daughters of the King of England still trickled in to the Court of St. James's from time to time. All, without exception, were rejected. None were even seriously considered. It was after a particularly trying incident involving an offer for Augusta from the old Landgrave of Hesse-Homburg, when Papa had literally foamed at the mouth, ranting against what he termed the Landgrave's infernal presumption, that Sophia and her lover had contrived to make one of their secret assignations. He, having come to Kew with other Cabinet ministers and Members of Parliament to confer with the King about Napoleon Bonaparte's latest *coup d'état* and the establishment of a Consulate in France, had managed to convey a message to her via her waiting-woman. That same night, Sophia, a cashmere shawl covering her thin gauze dress, had slipped out of the Queen's House and had run all the way to the Chinese pagoda. There he waited for her, his boots drumming an impatient tattoo on the marble floor. Crouched together on the bottom step of the huge, winding staircase, the two had discussed their desperate situation, Sophia bravely indicating her determination to free her lover, in order that he might 'look in another direction'. There was, she had declared shakily, fighting back the gathering tears, not the remotest possibility that they could ever achieve happiness together. He had silenced this noble offer with a kiss. He would remain faithful to her for ever, like the knights in the old romances, who worshipped their ladies from afar, yet might never possess them. The pious conceit did not enchant Sophia. She remembered Royal's *crie de coeur*, 'I need a man!' Shamelessly she had exploited her femininity, rubbing herself against him, inviting him to touch her neck, loosing her fichu so that he might explore the smooth white globes hitherto modestly concealed. He followed her lead, ignoring the warning signals flashing in his brain, oblivious to everything save her unashamedly offered body. She was a princess, he a commoner, but they might have been Jack and Jill mating in a haystack.

He had taken her with a violence not inherent in his nature, the anticipation of three years erupting into an emotion which he did not at first recognize as rage, a near-murderous intent, directed in paradox against the object of his affections, who was so far removed from him that he could never hope to acknowledge her openly as his wife. She, hurt and bruised, sensing something amiss as he lay panting in the dust of the dark, soaring pagoda, his white stock rising and falling within an inch of her nose, had questioned him fearfully. 'My dearest, you do still love me?'

He was instantly contrite, ashamed of himself for causing her a moment's unease. 'I love you with all my heart, darling Sophie.' His voice broke and he coughed to cover his weakness. 'Pray God we may find happiness,' he finished hoarsely.

'Please God,' she had murmured, stroking his hand, but she had not believed that they ever would.

Afterwards, of course, had come the reckoning, the worry when she missed her period, the utter refusal to acknowledge the frightening possibility that she might be pregnant, the sickening awful realization that the roundness of her belly was due to something more than chronic flatulence. She had actually quickened before she would admit to herself that she was with child.

One morning she had stood before her mirror, staring at her swelling abdomen and experiencing the onset of sheer terror. Without giving herself time to think any further, she had run, panic-stricken to tell her mother. The Queen, after paling visibly, had remained unaccountably calm. Had she not told herself long ago that just such a calamity might be looked for if the natural instincts of her daughters were callously ignored? All the same, it was undeniably a shock when the thing she had come to dread most actually assumed recognizable form. She had posed the all-important question, and Sophia had told her the name of the child's father. Charlotte had lifted her hands in despair, 'God in Heaven, could you not have chosen your paramour more wisely?' The Queen's unnatural calmness had deserted her then, to be replaced by indignation and anger that one of her daughters should have so far forgotten her high birth as to mate with a commoner.

'You are no better than George's wife,' she accused bitterly, 'with her *ménage* at Blackheath, or should I say menagerie? She too consorts with politicians, or so I have heard. She has now taken to adopting waifs and strays, the children of dockers and farmworkers. Perhaps you admire and would like to emulate such a one as she? I wonder that you do not start a nursery here at Kew.'

Sophia had winced at her mother's heavy sarcasm, at the same time conceding that Mama was entitled to her display of temper. She must wait patiently until it had run its course. It did not take long to do so, evaporating in an anxious, ever-present desire on Charlotte's part to spare the King worry and pain. Soon she was busying her mind with thoughts of the necessary arrangements which would have to be made.

It was eventually decided that Sophia, already five months' pregnant, must go to Weymouth, with one of her sisters among her attendants, and stay there until the child was born. A reliable midwife and an accoucheur would be engaged to supervize the birth, and the child would then be fostered out to a decent family in Weymouth — there were many such in that town who would willingly serve the Royal family in such a matter, remaining loyally discreet in return for a more than generous annual pension — and the whole unfortunate affair could then be forgotten. For the necessary few who must be made party to Sophia's disgraceful secret, a 'father' would be named to take the responsibility for having planted his seed in the body of a princess of the blood, some equerry of the King's, perhaps, who would allow his devotion to be stretched to breaking point and admit paternity of Sophia's child. Sophia had seen the advantages in such a plan. Her beloved would be ruined if the truth were made known and she would have died rather than bring disgrace on his head. A promising career in politics was opening up before him, and it was only fair that he should be allowed to pursue that career. Mama, however, had not been concerned about the fate of her daughter's ravisher, only that Sophia should not be thought to have fornicated with such as he. 'General Garth, I think, may be regarded as suitable to oblige the King in this respect,' she had decided. Sophia evinced some alarm. 'But he is fifty, if he is a day, and the ugliest man alive with that purple wen on his face.' She had started to weep. 'Oh, Mama, I shall be a laughing-stock!'

Charlotte had drawn her brows together in a formidable frown. 'None will presume to laugh at the King's daughter, at least not openly,' she promised grimly. 'General Garth will do very well. You will have cause to be grateful to him for shielding you against the opprobrium of the world.'

'But his station is no higher than that of . . .'

'He is the King's equerry,' her mother interjected before her daughter could utter the name of one who must now be erased from her mind. Sophia had been quite unable to see the logic of this, but she had made no further demur. Timidly she had asked, 'Shall you tell Papa? Please, Mama. I could not bear to do so.'

Mama had eyed her sternly. 'No, it is

not so agreeable having to own up and take the consequences for one's reckless behaviour, is it, my dear,' and then, her daughter's miserable countenance making her relent a little, 'I shall reveal everything to Papa after you have departed for Weymouth. By the time you return perhaps he will have forgiven you.'

'I . . . I had thought . . . ' ventured Sophia, determined to make one last bid for freedom.

'Yes?' Mama's tone had been forbiddingly sharp, so Sophia had rushed on before her courage failed her. 'I had thought we might be allowed to marry,' she finished breathlessly.

Mama had stared at her with slightly parted lips, like the principal character in a *tableau vivant* who has been instructed to 'look natural'. Then, not deigning to reply, she had thrown back her head and roared with laughter, dashing her daughter's hopes for ever. The die was cast, the game lost.

★   ★   ★

The ancient vehicle jogged along on its painful way. Sophia would have liked to remove her velvet pelisse, for the wet summer weather was sultry, and the interior of the coach, with its human heating agents, had become musty and hot. She was, however, reluctant to display her increasing bulk before her perceptive little niece, who was sure to comment upon it. She therefore sat and endured and occasionally allowed tears of self-pity to bedew her cheeks. Charlotte, bored with the sights of the English countryside, was staring at her accusingly. 'Your eyes are raining, Aunt Sophie. Are you unhappy?'

Mrs. Udney shushed her charge and Mary, once more immersed in her novel, looked up to say severely, 'Be silent, Charlotte. You are very naughty today. I do not know what we shall do with you.'

'You must *soot* me,' responded the irrespressible Charlotte. 'Papa says that all bad people are *sot*.'

* * *

The beach at Weymouth presented an unexciting spectacle. As far as the eye could see there stretched a hot, shimmering nothingness, composed of pebbles, sand and a brilliant blue sea. It being a hot day, the princesses had ordered their coachman to deposit flowered parasols and satin cushions in the lee of a wooden groyne, which afforded them some protection from the sun. Apart from the royal ladies, the only inhabitants occupying the stretch of beach fronting the large stone house which accommodated them during their stay, were Mrs. Udney, the Punch and Judy man and the toffee-apple woman. Far away to the left could be seen one of the new bathing machines, painted a bright yellow and drawn by a large grey horse. Leading the horse was a decently black-clad female attendant. The princesses had yet to sample the delights of sea bathing. Papa seemed to be having some difficulty in deciding whether or

74

not it was a proper pastime for his daughters. As Mary had suggested hopefully, 'If only we can persuade Papa that it is *healthful*, I think he may agree to it.' This was at least something to look forward to, a bright future promise to enrich the dull mediocrity of their lives.

The toffee-apple woman, having served the needs of the princesses, was trundling away her scarlet-painted cart with its proud, flaunting coat-of-arms emblazoned on the side, to indicate that its owner was patronized by none other than His Majesty King George III of England. The artist employed by the old woman to decorate her cart, had charged her the sum of 6d. for his work, but being somewhat lacking in heraldic knowledge, he had deposited the royal lions in the second and fourth quarters of the coat, a fact which afforded His Majesty a great deal of sly amusement. A kindly man, George had refused to allow anyone to tell the old woman of this heinous mistake, with the result that the Earl Marshal of England became a permanent insomniac, and Garter King of Arms dreamed nightly of wrongly quartered coats.

Princess Charlotte sunk her sharp white teeth into an enormous apple, thickly coated with rich brown toffee, and gestured at the red and white striped pavilion housing the Punch and Judy man, through the opening of which the garishly attired puppets could be seen, inanimate yet sinister, waiting to frighten and titillate. 'Mr. Punch is ready, Aunt Sophie,' she trilled. 'Please let us go and see!' So saying she seized Sophia by the hand, dragged her to her feet and plunged off in the direction of the pavilion. Mary stayed put with a book, waving a languid hand at her sister and niece, but Mrs. Udney, ever mindful of her duty, gallantly trudged along behind, wincing as the sharp pebbles of the beach cut into the thin soles of her fabric shoes.

Sophia screwed up her eyes against the onslaught of the sun and stared out to sea, where a tiny skiff struggled bravely against a brisk south-westerly wind blowing in from France. Her eye was caught by the sun-dappled, curling wavelets, dancing in towards the shore with skittishly upturned 'petticoats' and she was reminded of a row of dancing girls whom she had once glimpsed inside the covers of a forbidden magazine smuggled into Kew by one of her younger brothers. She had not imagined that the female leg could look so elegant in stockings. The gently moving sea, deceptively innocuous, had a hypnotic effect upon her, and she stood like one in a trance, admiring the gold-faceted waves, until Charlotte tugged impatiently at her hand and forced her back to reality.

Sophia sat down on a small canvas chair, thoughtfully provided by Mr. Punch's operator, and Charlotte settled beside her, still chewing on her toffee-apple, her small mouth ringed with sticky caramel. Sophia sighed, closing her eyes against the bright day.

Now that it was all over she could not shake off a strange sense of loss. It was as though she was still waiting for something to happen, waking each day to an aching emptiness, a void which was never filled, never would be filled, for it was an irrecoverable part of herself that eluded her.

The baby had been taken from her immediately after its birth, and she so dazed with copious doses of laudanum that she had not been sure whether the midwife had proclaimed it a boy or a girl. She had not held it in her arms, nor given it suck, nor yet inspected its face for a likeness to her beloved. Why then, did she feel so deprived, so bewildered and depressed? The child was nothing to her. The whole, night-marish episode might never have been.

Sophia had not dreamed that the nervous anticipation of childbirth would be so far removed from the reality. She had supposed, Mama having borne so many children, that the business was no more hazardous or complicated, no more painful than an attack of gout or measles. In retrospect she judged it to be fortunate that her imagination had not pictured the stark horror of that grinding pain which had gripped her body in a vice, mounting and receding, for hour after hour. Perhaps she was merely feeling cheated that she had nothing to show for all that agony. Sophia preferred this more prosaic interpretation of the involved emotional processes going on inside her. It relieved her of the necessity for deeper thought.

The Punch and Judy man, seeing his illustrious audience expectantly assembled and waiting with polite interest for the performance to begin, bobbed down, popped up again and deposited his little dog Toby, frilled collar and all, on to the 'stage', whereupon it promptly bit Mr. Punch's big red nose. The puppets became galvanized into action and thus began the sorrowful saga of Mr. Punch's domestic troubles. Charlotte, transfixed with delicious fright, drew her knees up to her chin, exposing a terrifying length of frilled drawers, and shrieked her appreciation as Mr. Punch assaulted his wife and the baby, outwitted the beadle, the undertaker and the devil, hung the hangman in his own noose, and succumbed at last to the machinations of Joey the clown. Surely, thought Sophia, it must have been a man who invented the story of Judy's trials and tribulations? She watched the macabre spectacle through to the end, covering Charlotte's eyes as Mr. Punch met his fearful deserts. Charlotte, tears streaming down her face as she mentally reviewed the woeful tragedy which had just been enacted before her, said tremulously, 'I enjoyed the play very much indeed, Aunt Sophie.' Sophia smiled, thanked and paid the creator of all these cunning devices, and the day being fair, decided to persuade her sister to stay and enjoy the sea air for another hour until it was time for lunch.

Mrs. Udney, sweltering in her governess's gown of black bombazine, her surprising green eyes keenly observant of all that went on about her, noticed that Her Royal Highness, the Princess Sophia was looking a trifle wan, and offered to take the boisterous Charlotte for a walk, to see if the donkey man was about. Both Sophia and Mary received and accepted this offer gratefully and sank on to the cushions under the groyne. The Punch and Judy man, his folded pavilion on his back, his puppets, imprisoned and lifeless inside a green felt bag, waved to them as he went by. They waved back, blessing the informality of this place so far removed from London, where a man of low degree might pass them without so much as the briefest of bows.

Mary yawned and stretched her arms over her head. She removed her straw bonnet with its knots of green ribbons and flung it from her, shaking out her fair curls. 'What a relief it is to be free,' she remarked lazily. 'No Mama. No ladies, except dear Mrs. Udney and the maids. No music or drawing lessons.'

'And no baby any more,' finished Sophia flatly.

Mary turned to look at her sister, a worried expression clouding her eyes. She clucked sympathetically as she observed Sophia's forlorn air. 'You could not have kept him, Sophie.'

'No.'

The two, so like each other in face and form, so near in age — but a year separated them — regarded each other in mournful silence. Then Sophia's eyes filled with tears and she turned her head away. Mary reached over to take her hand. 'We shall be returning to London next week, dearest,' she comforted. 'You will soon forget your dreadful experience.'

Sophia's head jerked round. The pallor of her cheeks frightened Mary. 'Forget?' whispered Sophia. 'How, pray, am I to forget? What is there to *make* me forget? Musical evenings with Mama and Papa? Listening to Lady Harcourt reading from the Bible every Sunday evening? Going to the theatre to watch dull plays considered suitable for our maiden ears? The piebald popovers?' She crammed her clenched fist into her mouth, biting her knuckles so hard that she drew blood. 'Jesus, I could scream!'

A deep, anxious frown creased Mary's brow. 'Papa may relent, my dear. *I* still have hopes of marriage.'

'Then you are a fool, *my dear*!' snapped Sophia.

Nettled by the sharpness of her sister's retort, Mary boasted, 'Our cousin William has been mighty attentive to me lately. At Mama's drawing-room in February he sat beside me and we conversed quite freely. Mama did not send Lady Harcourt to separate us.'

Sophia could not conceal her astonishment. 'Silly Billy? I thought you detested him?'

Mary picked at the bows decorating her sleeve. 'He is better than nothing.'

'There, dearest sister, you are quite wrong,' returned Sophia, wiping her eyes. 'Quite the contrary is the case. *Nothing* is better than Silly Billy. I daresay he wants you because he is only half royal and you will make him wholly so. At least,' she amended, 'you will make his children wholly royal.'

Mary sighed. 'I should so much like to have children.'

'So should I.'

'Oh, Sophie. You will have others. You will. I know Papa will change his mind when he sees us all so miserable.'

Sophia clicked her tongue exasperatedly. 'But Papa does not think we *are* miserable. He believes we love him so much that we never want to leave him.'

'We do love Papa,' agreed Mary dutifully, 'but I for one shall continue to hope, and you may think me a fool if you please.'

Sophia relented in the face of her sister's pathetic defiance. 'I beg your pardon, Mary, for being so sharp with you.'

Mary smiled forgivingly and tactfully changed the subject. 'I wonder what Gussie and the others are doing now?'

'Something most fearfully exciting I shouldn't wonder,' replied Sophia with mischievous sarcasm.

Mary giggled. 'Gussie was so jealous when Mama chose me to come to Weymouth with you.'

Sophia could not help laughing. 'The Brigadier will doubtless console her. I believe Mama is to hold a drawing-room this week. That will make Gussie happy, for it is the only occasion on which she may meet her Brigadier openly. They will stand together holding hands and gazing into each other's eyes until Mama sends Lady Harcourt to separate them.' Sophia's mouth drooped. 'How I envy Gussie,' she sighed. 'She is too astute to make the same foolish mistake as I.'

'Was it foolish?' asked Mary with sudden perception. 'At least you have loved, Sophie, and know what it is to bear a child.'

'In time I have no doubt that I shall come to thank God for that small consolation,' agreed Sophia quietly.

The plodding figure of a small, patient grey donkey, with a little girl on its back, hove into view, beside it, the long-suffering Mrs. Udney, who was endeavouring to ensure that the wriggling Charlotte would not fall. Sophia shaded her eyes with her hand. 'I wonder whom Charlotte will marry?'

'A handsome German prince,' prophesied Mary opening her mouth into a gaping yawn. 'And she will have fifteen children, just like Mama.'

KEW

1804

The King sat at his walnut secretaire in his study, scanning the latest despatches from France. What he read did not please him. The despatches, written by his son William from Marseilles, informed him that Napoleon Bonaparte had been crowned Emperor of France, that he was preparing to annex Hanover — great God what an outrage! — and that England was in danger of imminent invasion by this impudent Corsican Corporal.

George pressed his fingers to his temples, trying to dispel the throbbing ache which had persisted since dawn and refused to be banished, even though he had taken thirty drops of laudanum, this quite against the advice of his physicians, who had warned him that an overdose of this powerful soporofic could result in a lingering, unpleasant death. The King's principal equerry, Colonel Dalkeith, regarded him sympathetically. 'I fear the news from Europe is not at all good, Your Majesty.'

George managed a dry laugh. 'That, my dear Dalkeith, is the understatement of the year. The news is horrible, and unless I have enough ships in my navy to blockade Bonaparte's ports, and yet more vessels to blast him out of the water, I fear we may have to put ourselves in a state of defence.' He rose to his feet, ponderous and clumsy, carrying wearily his weight of sixty-six years. A frock-coat of dark green wool — a colour advised by his eldest son to give the impression of a more slender outline — though generously cut, could not hide the cushions of fat padding his portly figure, which strained to burst through the confines of the silver brocade waistcoat and tight stockinet breeches. He had a habit now and then of removing his wig to scratch his balding head, and it was as if he took off and replaced ten years in the short time it took him to perform this action. Colonel Dalkeith was reminded of the old adage 'Clothes maketh the man', as he watched the King circle the room with jerky steps, his little feet making deep indentations in the thick-piled Aubusson carpet. The Colonel was damned if he liked the look of His Majesty. Fidgety as a pea on a drum. Of course, those plaguey despatches hadn't helped.

Pop-eyed with anxiety, the King re-seated himself at his desk and drew towards him a large coloured map of Europe. He beckoned to his equerry, stabbing with his forefinger at the map. 'My son William is here' — he pointed to Marseilles — 'and Edward is here,' the finger moved to Gibraltar. He paused consideringly, his eyes darting over the map, 'and Admiral Nelson is in charge of the Mediterranean fleet at Toulon. Do you think, Dalkeith, that it would be a good move to station Nelson off the Bay of Biscay?'

Colonel Dalkeith shook his neatly barbered head emphatically. 'I should not care to advise Your Majesty to leave the Mediterranean without a watchdog,' he said doubtfully. He added with a smile, 'Besides, Sir, if I know Lord Nelson, his object is not only to blockade Toulon, but to entice the French out to do battle. Best leave him where he is, sir.'

'Yes, yes,' agreed the King with an air of weariness. 'We'll leave all as it is at present . . . at present, hey? Hey?'

'I think it would be prudent of Your Majesty to do so.'

George gave two or three abrupt nods and passed his hand across his brow. An odd feeling of unreality, a sort of disorientation, was creeping over him, accompanied by a slight yet persistent dizziness. He shook his head in an effort to clear it. An unpleasant singing sensation invaded his ears. 'Defences,' he muttered, 'coastal defences. We must put up some towers along the south coast, look-out towers. Station infantry-men there, day and night. Don't want that damned corporal taking us by surprise.'

'Martello towers, Your Majesty?'

'Yes, yes. Deuced clever invention those. Yes, yes, Martello, Martello. Corsican fellow, what? Hoist him with his own petard as they say,' and as his equerry stared at him in bewilderment. 'You know, Dalkeith. Cape Martello in Corsica. Withstood a British siege in '94. Had one of those damned towers there, so they tell me. S'how they go . . . name . . . ' The singing sensation increased. His head felt as though it was about to explode. He rose unsteadily to his feet, jerking his handkerchief out of his capacious pocket.

Colonel Dalkeith viewed the red, perspiring face with mounting alarm. 'Your Majesty is unwell? Shall I send for your physicians?'

'No, no, no!' George glared at the Colonel irritably and waved the sugges-tion aside. 'Hot in here, devilish hot. Go for a drive. Send for m'coach. See m'daughter-in-law.' His face creased into an expression of comic misery. Dalkeith thought he looked like a thwarted baby as he shouted, 'M'coach, damn ye! I want m'coach! Now!'

Colonel Dalkeith hastened to the door, overcome by a sudden, appalling fear. He opened it upon the Queen, stepped back smartly, and bowed. Behind him the King was dancing a clumsy jig and carolling, 'I am going to Blackheath! to Blackheath! to Blackheath! . . . ' The Queen cast a single, horrified glance at him and fled to summon the physicians.

They could not stop him from going. He was, after all, the King, and though it had been necessary to lay violent, restraining hands on him sixteen years previously, this had only been done after a four-hour deliberation by the Privy Council, and he was not, at this stage, doing anything more than behave like an indecorous schoolboy. His speech, though rapid, was quite coherent; he did not try to undress the Queen in public; he remembered that the Prime Minister had audience with him that afternoon; and he passed Lady Pembroke by without so much as a flicker of interest.

So they let him go, the Queen with many misgivings and terror in her heart, the physicians with worried and puzzled expressions, because they feared that, like the last occasion, they would have no effective remedies with which to cure the King, but would stand helplessly by while servants pulled him in and out of hot baths until the 'malady', as it had come to be known, decided of its own accord to go away. All these learned men nurtured a secret fear that one day the malady would not pass away and that the King would remain in the twilight for ever.

* * *

The Princess of Wales was not unduly flustered when the King was announced. Unexpected visitors were welcomed at Blackheath with open arms, any diversion from the dull round of carriage driving, card-playing and gossip being considered very fortunate indeed. On one memorable occasion, the Princess had been so bored that she had driven her singlehanded phaeton at break-neck speed round and round the grounds of her house, reducing her ladies to tears and placing her own life at risk. This burst of energy — a sort of working out of her frustrations — she had discovered to be most beneficial in restoring her equanimity, but being of a good-natured disposition, and knowing that she had frightened her servants half to death, she had not repeated the experiment. She sat now on a Grecian couch, gowned in apricot-coloured velvet, exposing at least six inches of leg above incongruous pink boots, and waited to receive her father-in-law.

At thirty-six Caroline of Brunswick had lost what youthful bloom had once been hers. Her face had now assumed the somewhat bloated appearance of one who does not take enough exercise, who eats too much rich food, and who indulges a taste for a particular brand of Italian wine. In addition to the aforesaid vices, Caroline, in the privacy of her bedroom, smoked long black cheroots, which stained her indifferent teeth to a sickly yellow and made her breath offensive. No one had ever thought her beautiful, but her complexion as a girl had been fresh and clear, her eyes a brilliant blue and her hair the bright spun gold of her Brunswicker forbears. The complexion was now rouged into artificial youth, the eyes were red-veined and dull, and the hair remained bright only by virtue of frequent washings in camomile flowers. Caroline's features were large and rather mannish, but there was a certain gentleness of expression which redeemed and flat-tered. The most charitable thing that could be said of her was that she resembled a tired, overblown rose.

In the nine years since her marriage, Caroline had not seen her husband above two or three times a year. Her union with the Prince of Wales was in itself a biting commentary on the senseless machinations of her elders, for never, in the whole course of English history, had so ill-matched a couple been brought together for the purposes of procreation. She, for her part, would no doubt have tolerated him, forgiven him much, overlooked much, including his ever-changing mistresses, his heavy drinking and his obsessive passion for donning military uniforms. No doubt. But he had made it perfectly plain that he could, under no circumstances, tolerate her, and for that she could not forgive him. Whenever Caroline recalled her first meeting with her husband she could never prevent a hot rush of blood from warming her cheeks, because he had found her appearance so obnoxious that he had visibly recoiled and requested that Lord Malmesbury bring him a glass of brandy. 'Harris, I am not well. Pray get me a glass of brandy.' Those were his exact words, branded on her heart, horrid, pride-wounding words. In feeble retaliation she began the habit of referring to him as the Great Mahomet, and the Queen, who aided and abetted the Prince in his dislike of her, became the Old Begum. Not content with this, Caroline was irresponsibly encouraging her daughter Charlotte to use both of these nick-names. Only the King supported her cause, and that, Caroline suspected, was because she was the daughter of his sister, Augusta.

Caroline greeted the King effusively, rising to curtsey to him. He embraced her with equal warmth and flinging himself clumsily upon the sofa, bade her sit beside him, inquiring solicitously after her health. She admitted to being pretty fair, and he, with heavy jocularity, agreed that she was, both pretty and fair. She laughed boisterously, rang the silver bell which hung by a chain from her neck — an eccentricity attributable to her inherent laziness, which made it a bore to rise from a sitting position in order to summon a servant — and offered him a glass of Madeira wine which he graciously accepted.

George slid his arm along the seat of the sofa and leant confidentially towards her. 'He treats you badly, hey? Hey?' She, in little doubt as to who 'he' was, confirmed that he did indeed treat her badly. Of late, she confided, he had forbidden her to see her daughter more than once a month, and all because she had threatened to publish a condemnation of his behaviour towards her in the 'Morning Chronicle'. The King started with horror. 'It won't do, won't do, won't do, m'dear.'

Caroline silently confessed to being a little puzzled. She had never known the King to adopt this air of easy familiarity. He was usually so very correct in his demeanour. Admittedly he had always been kind to her. He was, in fact, the only member of the Royal family who deigned to visit her, but he had never before displayed quite this much *laissez-faire*. She came to the conclusion that he had probably drunk too much at lunch and determined to take advantage of his mellow mood to put forward one or two small petitions. The wine came and she poured the King a generous measure, smiling broadly, 'I know, dearest Majesty, that you vill alvays look after my interests. You vill make sure that I see my daughter as often as I choose.'

'Every day, every hour, every minute of every hour,' he assured her. 'Why do you not have her here to live with you?' He favoured her with a warm, expansive smile.

Caroline stared at him. She wondered whether he was teasing her, but the smile, fading into gentle vagueness was still there, and she decided that he must be in earnest. The King knew very well that his son did not think her a fit mother for their child. So strongly did he hold this opinion that he had set up an establishment for his daughter at Warwick House, a building set in the grounds of his town residence, Carlton

House. Even the King could not interfere in this arrangement. What if he should try? The mere possibility filled Caroline with childish glee. What a sensation that would cause! What an exciting interlude in the dreary monotony of her days. There would be questions in Parliament, long articles in the newspapers, scurrilous cartoons. With any luck she could make quite a thing of it. Caroline loved a *cause célèbre*. It would bring her to the notice of the public, who had already shown, by various demonstrations outside her house, that they sympathized with her plight and thought her husband a wretch and a blaggard for treating her so shamefully. She said eagerly, 'Vill you order George to let me haf my daughter, Majesty?'

George rotated his arms in the exaggerated manner of a jubilant child. 'Order him? I will lay the birch to his bottom if he does not obey me. The rascal shall not be allowed to get away with it.'

Caroline tried to picture her stout husband submitting to a birching, and succeeding quite well with the aid of her well-developed imaginative powers, shook with mirth. George began to laugh too, apparently catching her mood. He laughed so hard that a silver button popped on his waistcoat. Still laughing he fell to his knees and began to crawl across the floor in search of the button. Caroline's little dog, nose brushing the floor, rushed round him in circles yapping excitedly. George barked in precise imitation of the animal.

It was then that Caroline knew for sure that something was very wrong. She had heard all about the King's malady, having wormed the information out of her lady-in-waiting, Lady Charlotte Campbell, and she was in no doubt that she was witnessing a recurrence. She rang the bell again, this time with some agitation. It was answered by a footman whom she despatched immediately to fetch the King's coachman, dozing on the box outside. Between them, the three got the King to his feet and into the coach. Caroline, always at her best in a genuine emergency, instructed the coachman to take the King back to Kew and not to let him leave the vehicle until the equerries came out to receive him. Then she ran back into the house, seized pen and paper, and wrote to her dear friend, Sir Thomas Lawrence, the painter, to her dear friend, Richard Brinsley Sheridan, and to her dear friend, Lord Byron, informing them all that the King had tried to ravish her, but that fortunately she had fallen off the sofa before he could succeed in his dire purpose. Caroline found the next hour not at all boring.

★ ★ ★

The Prince of Wales having given orders that his sister was to be shown into the green and gold room of Carlton House, seated himself in a comfortable elbow chair to await her arrival, due, according to Augusta's letter, at ten o'clock precisely. Above his head the chandelier of Italian cut crystal — the second of its kind which had come by the sea route from Naples, the original having sunk to oblivion in a severe storm off the Bay of Biscay — swayed and tinkled in the light breeze filtering in through the open window, its prismed pendants turned by the sun's rays into blazing, coloured gems.

With a womanish moue of distaste, the Prince flicked at a minute speck of snuff which adhered to his frilled lace cuffs, then extracted the satin-lined tails of his crimson velvet frockcoat from under his spreading posterior, so that they would not show the slightest crease, reflecting as he did so that Brummell's tailor was certainly a master of his craft. But then he would hardly be patronized by the finest dandy in London were he anything less than perfect. The Prince often regretted having quarrelled with George Brummell, whose ready wit had so amused him. Unfortunately wit had degenerated into over-familiarity and insult, and Brummell had signed his own death warrant when he had referred to Maria Fitzherbert as 'Mistress' Fitzherbert, publicly humiliating her and sending her weeping from the room. For that breach of manners he would never be forgiven. He had, however, left behind him a generous legacy for his friend the Prince of Wales, who had once dressed indifferently well, but had now become an arbiter of what constituted masculine elegance, the personification of sartorial perfection, without a rival in the whole of Europe.

A long, gilt-framed pier glass reflected his solid image. He preened himself, adjusting the folds of his white stock, displaying his legs, of which he was inordinately proud, in their skin-tight trousers of fawn broadcloth. He thought that the new fashion of trousers showed off his calves to better advantage than the old-fashioned knee breeches, which broke up the line of the leg. The latter were now used only for formal occasions. His gaze travelled upwards, alighting finally on his face, which he thought still handsome, despite the fact that it had weathered forty odd years. It struck him as distinctly singular that the facial characteristics of the Hanoverian males continued to persist, generation after generation, the distaff side without power seemingly to transmute the protuberant eyes, the long, heavy noses and slack, sensual mouths into more delicate proportions. The notion diverted him. He caught sight of Lady Hertford tripping across the courtyard in the direction of Warwick House. She turned to wave to him and he waved back. He had requested her not to be present at his interview with Augusta because, as he put it, Gussie's letter was devilish odd, with its references to a 'personal matter, most secret'. Lady

Hertford had laughed. 'Tell me all about it afterwards, George. I shall pass the time by going over to Warwick House to talk to that most precocious imp of yours. I swear she looks more like you every day.'

He watched her running away from him, her skirts gathered in her hands, her fair hair blowing in the wind, and a sentimental tear trickled down his nose. She was so beautiful, his latest inamorata. How strange to think that he might never have been introduced to her had not dear Maria expressed a desire to adopt the infant daughter of Lord Hertford's brother by his first wife, little Minnie Seymour. Maria, who had so wanted a child of her own, and had been so desperately unhappy all those years ago when she had miscarried at Brighton. The Prince, who was a highly emotional man, was apt to regard women with the noble-minded, romantic view of the poets. Like the poets, he put them on a pedestal, from which, to his chagrin, they frequently fell.

Caroline, of course, was a prime example of the fallen goddess. From the very first she had refused to behave like his ideal of womanhood. She was slovenly in her dress, she talked loudly, she made *risqué* remarks, she picked her teeth in public, she offended. Maria Fitzherbert was perhaps the only woman he had ever known who lived up to his expectations. She was quiet and gentle, not beautiful, but always immaculate in her appearance, always so understanding. The Prince was a man of great intellect and varied interests, but he had in him a strong streak of immaturity, a little boy complex which required that there should always be a woman in his life to chide him gently when he was naughty and kiss him better when he was hurt. In return he treated all of them abominably, all that is except his mother and his sisters whose persons were sacrosanct.

The door opened, Gussie was

announced, and he rose to greet her. He saw, with a considerable start of surprise, that she was looking pretty handsome this morning in her fur-trimmed pelisse of dark blue velvet, with a blue satin bonnet to match. The latter detracted from her large nose and brought out the colour of her blue-green eyes. Her cheeks glowed with health and she was smiling gaily.

Her opinion of his looks, on the other hand, was far from flattering. She thought that her brother had put on some weight in the two months since she had last seen him, and there were bags under his eyes which had not been there before. He was more like Papa than ever. He strode towards her, took her by the hand and kissed her on both cheeks. 'Gussie, my dear, come and sit down. How pleasant it is to see you. You are looking very well.'

'And you, George, are looking the very picture of health,' she lied. Seating herself on a stiffly elegant example of Mr. Sheraton's work, she picked up a parasol negligently propped against it. 'Charming,' she remarked. 'I have not seen one of that particular colour before.' She started to examine the parasol, her fingers stroking the pale mauve silk. Hastily he took it from her and flung it behind a sofa, meeting her sardonic regard with a sheepish grin. 'It belongs to Lady Hertford,' he explained.

She nodded with apparent under-standing, observing amiably, 'I did not for one moment imagine that you were in the habit of carrying such an article, George.' Her steady gaze held his. 'There are times, George, when I wish most heartily that I had been born a man, a callous, unfeeling man, so that I might employ the services of any bitch of a whore who cared to cast her eye upon me.'

'Augusta!' If she had set out to shock him she had certainly succeeded. His eyes fairly bulged with horrified reproach. His expression of hurt accu-sation made her lose patience. 'Oh come, George. I am thirty-six years old. Do you think that I have progressed this far in life without picking up a few stable colloquialisms from my bevy of rumbustious brothers?'

Ignoring the gibe he replied primly, 'It does not sound well on you, Gussie.'

She shrugged indifferently. 'I came here to ask a favour of you, George.'

'Anything!' he offered extravagantly, only too pleased to be able to change the subject.

'If I were you, I should be inclined to display a little more caution until you have ascertained what it is I want.'

'Come along then, out with it.'

For a moment she hesitated. Now that the time had come, she feared that she would not have the courage to make her request, a fear only outweighed by the possibility that he might refuse her. Blunt by nature she was not able to phrase her petition in anything other than the most direct term. 'Now that Papa is mad,' she blurted, 'I want you to give me permission to marry Brigadier-General Brent Spencer.'

If she had asked to go to the moon he could not have been more astonished. He opened his mouth to object but before he could say a word she rose from her chair, crossed to where he sat, and flung herself upon him, her arms circling his neck. 'George, please. I beg you to help me. We will be very discreet. No one shall ever know.' She started to weep, resting her head on his shoulder. 'Father refused another offer for me before he became ill. Not that I should have wanted Ferdinand of Würtemberg. I should have had to live near Royal and she would have played the tyrant with me I daresay.' She laughed shakily and went on, 'If you will give your consent now, George, our marriage will be legal, and even if Papa does get better and finds out, he will not be able to have the marriage annulled like he did with Augustus, because I am of age. 'Oh, George,' she wailed, 'I want a proper marriage, not a hole-in-the-corner affair. I do not want to be anyone's mistress.'

Sparing a thought for his new frock-coat — velvet did not take kindly to salt water — the Prince gently disentangled himself and stood up, pressing his sister back into the chair. She looked up at him in piteous appeal and he felt his own eyes beginning to water. Nonetheless he managed to say steadily, 'You know that I cannot do as you ask, Gussie.' He moved away from her and went to stand by a round mahogany table, tracing with his forefinger its coloured ceramic medallions inset into the wood. He said: 'I do not suppose you remember much about Papa's illness. You were not very old at the time.'

'I was twenty.'

He smiled at the note of slight indignation in her voice. 'Well, that is not very old, my dear.' She was about to say something more, but he stayed her with a raised hand and continued,

'There was a great deal of to-do about the passing of a Regency Bill which would have given me sovereign powers. The politicians wrangled, at least the Tories did, Fred and I quarrelled, and before anything could be resolved, Papa did us all a favour by recovering.' Slowly he circled the table, still fingering the designs. 'This time the politicians are more cautious. They have adopted a 'wait and see' policy, and I have no more power than any other Privy Councillor. So you see, I cannot do as you ask.'

She was silent for a long time. When she did find her voice she spoke in a flat monotone, which all too clearly revealed her bitterness. 'I knew you would not help me. I knew I could not hope for happiness. I was a fool to ask you.'

He came towards her and touched her cheek with his finger. 'None of us can, Gussie. We are all trapped by an accident of birth, a quirk of fate if you like.'

'You manage very successfully to

circumvent the accident of your birth, George,' she retorted acidly. She had an unworthy desire to hurt him now that he had proved such a frail vessel. He gave no sign that the stinging words afforded him so much pain. 'You think I am happy, Gussie?' he asked mildly. She looked surprised. 'Are you not then? You are free to come and go as you please. You have limitless resources to indulge your somewhat exotic tastes,' a sweeping arm indicated the expensive furnishings, 'and you are not obliged to ask Papa whether you may or may not receive your friends.'

'I also have a wife who ridicules me in public and makes me look a fool in the eyes of Papa's subjects. I have a daughter instead of a son, few real friends and a host of sycophantic followers.'

She rose, rather stiffly, as though her limbs had suddenly aged. 'Well, George,' she said, 'I see you have no favours for me today. I shall tell Brigadier Spencer that I must play the whore. He may hope for little else, as my brother will have it so.'

After Augusta had taken her leave, presenting a cool, indifferent cheek for him to kiss, the Prince clenched his right fist and banged it into the palm of his left hand. 'Dam'me, Father,' he muttered, 'if I don't think ye really are mad!'

* * *

By the time Augusta had an opportunity of seeing her Brigadier again, the King was fully restored to health, and all was as it had been before. They met at one of the Queen's drawing-rooms which was being held in her audience chamber at Windsor. The two lovers stood together, as so often before, partially concealed from the company by a painted screen, and watched the parade of ladies and gentlemen bowing and curtseying before Charlotte.

'Well, my dear,' said Augusta, regarding her eagle tenderly, 'so you will have to make a dishonest woman of me at last. I think we have earned a small measure of happiness, you and I.'

He returned her look with equal tenderness. 'If that is your wish, sweetheart.'

'It is,' she replied firmly, and raised her glass of claret to the level of his eyes. 'To us,' she toasted. He signalled to a passing servant and removing a crystal goblet from the proffered tray, returned her toast. 'Can you try for an establishment of your own?'

She laughed up at him. 'Certainly I can try, but I fear I shall not succeed. No, my dear. You will have to rely upon my making assignations. Do not you think that shocking in an old woman of thirty-six?'

He sensed the deep hurt underlying the lightness of her tone and responded angrily, 'Certainly it is shocking, and how foolish we have been to deny ourselves for so many years that which is our right.'

She lowered her head, filled with a sudden sense of shame at her cowardice. 'I did not want to follow Sophie's example. If I had borne a child, I could not have endured to part with it.'

His stomach turned over at the thought of the anguish she must have suffered for his sake. In an attempt to raise her spirits he said teasingly, 'It is still possible you know.'

Her head shot up, eyes forlorn. 'No, no. I think not. Papa has seen to that. Is it not passing strange to think that we are thirteen in number, all grown to maturity, and Papa has but one legitimate grandchild?'

'Aye, it is passing strange,' he agreed, sighing deeply.

She saw that it was her turn to play the comforter and told him cheerfully, 'I am having my likeness painted in miniature by Mr. Beechey. I shall sit for him very demure in a white fichu with a kerchief covering my head. I am determined to look like a soldier's wife.' She was laughing now, but there were tears in her eyes. He took her hand. 'Dearest wife,' he said, and greatly daring, for the Queen's eye was upon them, he pressed her fingers to his lips.

WINDSOR

1808

The King could hardly contain his rage. He paced his study, his progress so rapid that Frederick, Duke of York, stationed at a safe distance, thought he might very well break into a run at any moment. Suddenly George rounded on his son, both arms flailing the air, fists clenched into threatening, white-knuckled weapons, and shrieked, 'Colonel Wardle! That nobody! He has risen in the House to request an investigation into the sale of Army commissions by that . . . that woman you cohabited with . . . that Mrs. Clarke!'

'But, Papa . . . ' Frederick started to protest, eyes blinking fiercely as his nervousness increased, actually recoiling when his father advanced upon him

119

pouring out words like a stream of molten lava. 'But nothing!' roared the King, and now a stabbing forefinger came within an inch of Frederick's third waistcoat button. 'These commissions,' George pursued relentlessly, 'were sold with your knowledge and consent. My own son, the Duke of York, stood by complacently while his whore sold commissions in *my army*! You have brought shame on me and on the uniform you wear as Commander-in-Chief. You are also a Bishop. Had you forgot that when you descended to the level of a common criminal? Eh? Eh? Had you forgot?'

Frederick, whose title of Bishop of Osnaburg caused him untold embarrassment, opened his mouth to defend himself and shut it again quickly as he felt his father's hot breath fanning his face. 'Not only Army commissions though, was it?' George bullied, 'Politicians have benefited from Mrs. Clarke's interfering finger; preachers have obtained licences to deliver sermons before me; aspirants to snug deaneries have been satisfied, on payment of a substantial bribe, of good livings.'

The King paused to suck in air, and thus fortified summed up his biting comments. 'Well, Sir, you will resign from your appointment, and your erstwhile mistress will have to appear before the Bar of the House of Commons to answer upon charges of bribery and corruption.'

'Resign, Papa?' Frederick's round red face looked honestly puzzled.

The King glared at this replica of his eldest son. Frederick was an exact copy of George in every way, even down to his damned tom-foolery with unsuitable women. He said heavily, 'You did not imagine that you could retain your post as Commander-in-Chief of the British Army after this?'

'A man is innocent until proved guilty, Papa,' Frederick replied sulkily and very unwisely.

The Hanoverian eyes bulged. 'Oh, so we are whiter than snow now, are we?

We did not know what Mistress Clarke was up to. We should have been shocked had we known her to be capable of such a thing, should we not?'

Frederick's eyes dropped to his boots. 'I knew about it, Papa. I did not think any harm could come of it.'

By his next remark the King displayed his amazing grasp of human frailty. 'Nor was much harm done,' he conceded. 'The undeserving rarely maintain positions of authority for long in my experience. No, your crime and hers is in being found out.'

Frederick almost laughed with relief, but the look on his father's face prevented him from doing anything so foolish. George did not think his observations in any way humourous. He had merely been stating a fact. 'Go home to your wife, Frederick,' he advised 'and live the simple, domestic life, as the Queen and I have done for nearly fifty years. It is time you stopped these tedious entanglements with women.'

Frederick shuddered at the thought of domesticity with Frederica, his German wife, who kept a menagerie at their house at Oatlands and ate sandwiches on the lawn at midnight. Relieved that the interview was over, he kissed the King's hand and withdrew.

Watching his son's broad, departing back, George sighed wearily and sat down at his desk. He was worried about his youngest daughter, the Princess Amelia, who had contracted a severe, feverish cold in late summer and had not been able to shake off the terrible racking cough which had accompanied it, and yet persisted, day after day. He would send her to Weymouth, he decided, even though it was out of season. The sea air might effect a cure. Perhaps Charles Fitzroy would act as her escort again. A solid, respectable young man that, always willing to look after Amelia. Knew his place though. Wouldn't presume. Damned if that business with Fred hadn't given him a headache. Stupid fool . . . damned

woman . . . how they plagued him, these
sons of his. Always having to get them
out of scrapes. At first it had been his
brothers, now it was his sons . . . God,
but his head was pounding . . . get the
Queen . . . laudanum . . . felt dizzy too.
So much to do . . . couldn't give in . . .

★ ★ ★

Colonel the Honourable Charles Fitzroy of the Third King's Own Hussars,
spurred his stallion into a gallop, and
streaked along the sands after the
bolting mare and rider already several
lengths in front of him. An old woman,
engaged in the making of lobster pots,
yelled abuse as a shower of wet sand,
thrown up by the stallion's pounding
hooves, spattered her face, stinging her
eyes and nostrils. Spewing invective, she
shook her fist at the military gentleman
and bent to retrieve her fallen willow
sticks. The young man heard but did not
heed as he bent low over the animal's
glossy neck, his pride as well as his

position at stake if he did not catch up with the Princess before she came to grief.

Half a mile of hard riding and the mare's rump, dangerously lathered, was within an inch of his stallion's nose and then he was alongside, his hand on the mare's bridle, pulling her up so sharply that what he had feared most, nearly came to pass. The Princess Amelia let out a howl of fright, recovered expertly, then burst into peals of laughter, turning towards her pursuer a face flushed with excitement. 'Lord, Charles!' she exclaimed, quite out of breath and choking on her mirth, 'I vow you look as though you'd seen a ghost.'

He stared at her accusingly. 'You did it on purpose,' he said indignantly. 'You threw down that piece of paper to make her bolt.'

She was laughing so hard, flinging back her head, that her plumed riding bonnet fell off, releasing her long blonde hair. His mischievous brown eyes took on the light of battle. Drawing his sword, he manœuvred his horse into position and nudged it into skittering sideways towards the errant bonnet. She screamed in protest as he speared the confection of velvet and ribbon and offered it to her with a ceremonious bow. She pouted at him. 'Oh, Charles, that is mighty ungallant of you. I adored that bonnet.'

Having punished, he was ready to placate, his masculine superiority re-established. 'I shall buy you a thousand bonnets, Ma'am, so that you may have a new one every day for three years.'

She elevated her eyebrows with studied effect. 'On a Colonel's pay, sir?'

He looked aggrieved. 'It is cruel of Your Highness to remind me that I am so far beneath you.'

She blew him a kiss in compensation and sliding easily from the mare's back, ran towards the sea. He trotted after her, leading the mare, and dismounting, tied the two horses to a groyne.

Amelia sat down on a withered tree

stump in the lee of a small tarred fishing smack, upon which several nets had been draped to dry in the sun. She looked up, patting the pebbles beside her, inviting him to come and join her, which he did with the utmost willingness, for he was deeply in love with this fair, delicate creature from the royal harem. It had been Amelia herself who had told him of her sisters' secret name for the household at Kew, so predominantly feminine. It amused him a good deal, especially when she referred to the Queen as the Keeper of the Harem and to the footmen as the royal eunuchs.

Charles Fitzroy was himself connected to the royal line, being a descendant of King Charles II by that king's liaison with Barbara Palmer. Born on the wrong side of the blanket, he had all the 'pretender's' respect for the genuine article and realized, better than Amelia perhaps, the yawning gulf which separated their two lives. He was not at all displeased when his friends laughingly called him 'Prince Charles'.

Amelia was fumbling in the pocket of her blue velvet habit and to his surprise brought forth a crumpled sheaf of papers which she proceeded to spread out on her lap. Idly he questioned her. 'What is that? A letter from a secret admirer?' She grinned up at him, batting her eyelids, teasing, inviting, making him wish that he could embrace her, not at all gently, and do with her what he had done a hundred times before.

'This, my dear,' she said archly, 'is a solemnly-worded document which must be taken very seriously indeed. I have read every word of it and I can tell you that it made my head ache.' She giggled girlishly, 'At the same time it gave me great cause for hope.'

She had succeeded in arousing his curiosity. 'What *is* it?' He made a grab for the papers, but she was too quick for him. Shrieking with laughter, she snatched them away. He, being the more accomplished strategist of the two, now pretended indifference and picking up some smooth, flat stones, began throwing them into the sea, congratulating himself aloud as they skimmed over the placid water. This little ploy was immediately successful, for Amelia could not bear to be cold-shouldered. 'It is a copy of the Royal Marriage Act of 1772,' she declared importantly. 'Lord Chancellor Eldon had it copied for me by one of his clerks, and mighty curious he was to know why I wanted to peruse such a document, though he must have guessed something of the truth.'

His heart missed a beat. Had she really been serious then, when she had hinted at marriage before they left Kew? He suffered a sharp twinge of conscience. The King trusted him, enough to allow him to accompany Amelia on rides and walks without the stifling presence of chaperones. He had betrayed that trust, right from the very first day, seven years ago now, when the King had appointed him as the princess's guardian for the period of her holiday at Weymouth. True, they had been accompanied to the seaside resort by the princesses Mary and Elizabeth and their ladies, not to mention two coachmen, a laundress and the princess's physicians, but for all the notice they took of these companions and servants they might have been non-existent. Amelia and Charles had had eyes only for each other and on several occasions they had managed to slip away alone to talk and talk, and hold hands, and dream impossible dreams. In the space of a single day they had become soul-mates, spiritual lovers. In the space of a week they had begun to enjoy the more complete and satisfying contact of physical love. They had been made for each other it seemed, and yet he had not dared to hope that he might ever marry her. He said, as nonchalantly as excitement would allow, 'And why do you wish to peruse such a document?'

She leaned towards him, speaking

eagerly, her light blue eyes communicating an intensity of purpose which boded well for their cause. 'Charles, dearest, I have read this through again and again, and it seems that after the age of twenty-five, any member of the Royal family may marry whom he or she pleases, provided that twelve months' notice of intention to marry is given to the Privy Council.'

'Surely only if that person is approved by the King?' he demurred.

'There is no such stipulation contained in the provisions of this Act,' she replied quickly. With an air of suppressed excitement she read out the relevant passage: 'Descendants of His Majesty, King George the Second (except the issue of princesses married into foreign families) may not marry without the sovereign's consent. Any marriage made without such consent shall be declared null and void. Descendants over the age of twenty-five, however' — Amelia paused significantly and raised her eyebrows with great dramatic effect — 'may marry without the sovereign's consent, provided twelve months' notice is given to the Privy Council and both Houses of Parliament do not expressly declare their disapproval.' Amelia folded the papers and said firmly, 'As soon as we return to Kew I shall write to Spencer Perceval, our revered Prime Minister, and declare my intention to marry Colonel the Honourable Charles Fitzroy of the Third King's Own Hussars.'

Elation gave way to deflation. 'A whole year to wait!' he lamented.

She studied him intently, surprised by his look of real anguish. 'Charles, I believe you really do love me.'

His gaze signified astonished stupefaction. 'Can you doubt it?'

She placed both hands on her reddening cheeks. 'I thought . . . I mean I . . . ' Amelia's voice faltered, then she rushed on in confusion, 'I was so forward, Charles, and sometimes I wondered whether you responded from a desire not to offend the King's daughter. It did cross my mind that perhaps you were merely being . . . polite to me.'

'Polite? Polite! God save us!' He guffawed so loudly that a seagull, perched on the groyne, took off in offended fright. Amelia laughed, uncertainly at first, then more whole-heartedly as she realized the extent of her *faux-pas*. He pulled her down to him and held her close, kissing her eyes, her hair, her nose and last of all her mouth, to which he clung as though his life depended upon it.

She was the first to break away, seized by a fit of coughing which shook her body and made her eyes water. She put her hands to her breast, rocking back and forth while he voiced his concern. 'You are not yet well, Amelia. I have been so happy here at Weymouth that I have quite forgotten that you came here to recuperate from an attack of influenza. I am a selfish brute to have kept you out so long today. We shall return at once.' Gently he patted her back as she spluttered, 'You are going to marry an invalid, Charles.'

'My loving will make you well again.'

'Yes, oh yes.' Amelia was crying with happiness now. She wiped her eyes on her sleeve and said determinedly, 'We shall not wait for a year, Charles. I shall give notice to the Privy Council, but we shall marry straight away and reveal our secret when the twelve months are up. Our little ruse will not alter the legality of the marriage.'

'But if we are discovered, we shall get ourselves into a packet of trouble,' he objected doubtfully.

Her mouth tightened stubbornly. 'I am twenty-six, Charles. I want my husband to be acknowledged before the world and I want my children at my side, unremarkable things which Papa has so far denied to me and to my sisters. Have you forgot that I bore you a daughter last year, a daughter who was torn from my arms and fostered out with poor Sophie's son? Does it not anger you, Charles, to think that our child is with common people, when she should be recognized as a Princess of England?' Her eyes flared into anger. 'I have always been an obedient daughter to Papa, and of all his children I think he loves me best. If he knew what I was about to do it would hurt him dreadfully, but I shall do it all the same.'

He was still troubled, though mention of his baby had stiffened his own resolution. 'Who will marry us?'

She laughed. 'That is no problem, my dear. We shall go to the parish of Upwey — it is only five or six miles away from here — enter the church, and giving false names, pay the parson to make us man and wife. If Gussie had any sense she would do the same. She loathes being without that little slip of paper which would bind her legally to her Brigadier. I vow and declare that to feel as guilty as she must quite take the pleasure out of loving. Did you know, Charles, that you look exactly like Samuel Cowper's portrait of King Charles the Second?'

'Do I?'

'You know you do, you coxcomb,' she teased. 'What a situation, my dear. A descendant of Old Rowley about to marry a descendant of the Hanoverian usurper!'

'Hush, sweetheart,' he cautioned, finger to lip, but laughing nonetheless. 'That is treason.'

A seagull, perhaps the same that had flown away protestingly from noisy humanity, circled overhead, wheeled and swooped down upon a small crab which had unwisely left the shelter of its rocky pool. A large blob of bird-lime was deposited upon the Colonel's immaculate white breeches. Amelia shrieked her delight. 'That's your escutcheon blotted, Prince Charles!'

THE PAVILION, BRIGHTON

1810

Lady De Clifford, governess to the Princess Charlotte, faced the Prince of Wales across a vast expanse of Persian carpet. The delicacy of her mission, coupled with the possibility that she might arouse the Prince's anger, made her tremble with apprehension, a feeling which was not helped by the fact that he was staring at her with a kind of fixed hostility as though he sensed that she was about to impart uncomfortable news. The stern, Puritanical eye of the governess was offended by the eastern exotica with which she was surrounded. The Prince had received her in the Rotunda, the principal apartment in the Pavilion, the walls of which were hung with papered panels representing a

Chinese formal garden a-blaze with flowering trees, shrubs, flowers, birds and butterflies, perfectly offset by a yellow background. The domed ceiling of this remarkable chamber represented a cloudy sky, in the centre of which was a huge golden star with silvered fish appearing between its rays. Round the base of the cupola was a carved and gilded cornice with pendant bells. Five gold-framed pier-glasses alternated with the papered panels in a vast, glittering circle. The doors, closed now to exclude listening ears, were of English lacquer work. All this magnificence went unappreciated by Lady de Clifford, who thought it a monstrous extravagance, and marvelled not at all that the Prince's debts were causing another spate of questions to be asked in Parliament and were helping to drive the King towards the brink of inevitable, permanent insanity.

Embarrassed by his Highness's steady, unblinking gaze, Lady de Clifford looked down at her mittened hands and wished heartily that she was safely enclosed in her coach and on her way back to London, but the interview must begin somehow, even if such banalities as the weather must be discussed before the main object of her visit could be touched upon. So, with a clearing of her throat and an unnecessary adjustment of her carefully disposed skirt, Lady de Clifford remarked pleasantly that it being November, one would have expected the weather to be somewhat less clement.

The Prince, ever courteous, a past-master at the art of exchanging preliminary generalities, agreed at some length that one would indeed, and then fell silent again. Lady de Clifford allowed his superiority in the matter of opening gambits, cleared her throat a second time, and said with unaccustomed directness, 'I greatly fear, Your Highness, that the Princess Charlotte is giving us, her ladies, some cause for concern.'

The Prince tilted his head to one side

inquiringly, his brows drawn together in a puzzled, anxious frown. 'I had not heard that my daughter was indisposed?'

'No, no, Your Highness.' Lady de Clifford hastened to dispel any worries on that score. 'I assure you that Her Highness is in excellent health and spirits.'

'Then I fail to see . . . ?'

Lady de Clifford's hands began to perspire. With a great effort of will she forced herself to make the shocking revelation. 'It has become apparent that Her Royal Highness has fallen into evil company.'

The royal eyebrows shot up as the Prince gave a short, disbelieving laugh. 'I do not comprehend how that could possibly be, Lady de Clifford, unless you and the other ladies have been extremely remiss in your duties.'

She was filled with indignation. At least he might wait until he had heard the whole story before he began to condemn the members of his daughter's household. She said stiffly, 'There are none at Warwick House, Your Highness, who have been remiss. I refer to the fortnightly visits made by Her Royal Highness to the Princess of Wales at Blackheath.' Let him chew on that!

He did, and came to the conclusion that the matter was rather more serious than he had at first imagined. True, he had been somewhat startled to learn that the governess had travelled all the way from London, to see him, but he had not thought that she would reveal anything more dreadful than a servants' quarrel. Upon hearing that his wife was involved, however, he was immediately on the alert. His eyes narrowed. 'You had better explain, Ma'am.'

She did not find it easy to meet him eye to eye, but steeled herself to do so. She was performing her duty as she saw it, and if he chose to blame her for the whole unfortunate business, let him, and she would resign her post and be glad. The Princess Charlotte was a wilful, boisterous girl, difficult to control, and with too much of her mother in her for her own good. 'It appears,' she began, with what she hoped was a daunting degree of coolness, 'that the Princess of Wales is in the habit of inviting young military gentlemen to her house for the express purpose of providing a diversion for Her Royal Highness.'

A dangerous bulging of the blue eyes made her rush on, eager to get her tale done before an explosion of wrath unnerved her completely. 'At first I thought there was little harm in Her Royal Highness riding in the grounds of Blackheath House with one of these young men, since they were always chaperoned by two or three of the ladies of the household, but on returning from one of her visits to her mother the Princess informed me that she had been permitted to converse with one of the young gentlemen unchaperoned, the Princess of Wales having locked them into one of the bedrooms in the house bidding them 'amuse themselves'.'

'Hellfire!'

Lady de Clifford held her breath, impaled by that dreadful Hanoverian stare, and then was witness to a slow and strange transformation. The eyes, so to speak, 'subsided', the rigid, offended posture was relaxed, and a small, one might almost say sly smile, curved the loose mouth. With an air of triumphant justification the Prince said, 'I always had misgivings about permitting my daughter to visit that woman. His Majesty thought me unfeeling in my treatment of her who I am reluctant to call my wife, but he does not know her as I do.' He began to work himself up to a pitch of righteous indignation which Lady de Clifford knew to be feigned, since he was so obviously enjoying himself. 'The woman is mad. I have always said so. They had no right to marry the heir to the throne to an irresponsible, reckless, ill-mannered slut! I shall not permit her to see my daughter. This is the end, the end! Henceforth the Princess Charlotte shall live with the Queen at Windsor for at least six months of the year. For the rest, she may reside at Warwick House, with twice-yearly visits to Weymouth to receive the benefits of the sea air.'

He ranted on, dragging up past grievances, raking over the dead ashes of the inquiry which had been conducted, four years previously, into the conduct of the Princess of Wales, who had been accused by the malicious Lady Douglas, her one-time friend, of taking various men as her lovers, and of having borne an illegitimate child. Since Caroline, with her awkward sense of fun, had stuffed cushions under her gowns to 'encourage that great repeater, Lady Douglas, to make an ass of herself', the gossip-mongers were not entirely to be blamed, but the Delicate Investigation as it had been styled, had achieved nothing beyond branding the Prince a callous husband and an unnatural father, and the Princess a martyr.

The Prince had never forgiven those

who had carried out the investigation on his behalf for not pronouncing his wife guilty of adultery and permitting him to divorce her. Now, with this saga of evil-doing from the lips of Lady de Clifford, he felt himself to be on firmer ground. They would all see that he had been right about that vile woman.

After bidding Lady de Clifford an unexpectedly gracious farewell, the Prince of Wales told Maria Fitzherbert that he must return to London at once, pondering as he did so upon the advisability of abandoning Maria for good and making a serious effort to establish a favourable public image as an injured husband and a devoted father.

* * *

When the Prince reached London, after two hours' hard driving in his carriage, thoughts of his wife and daughter were temporarily dispelled by the disquieting intelligence that his youngest sister was lying dangerously ill at Windsor. He went at once to the castle to see her and found to his dismay that the physicians had by no means overstated the case when they had described her condition as giving grave cause for alarm.

Hurrying to his sister's apartments, the Prince came upon his father, distraught and weeping copiously, slumped over Amelia's bed and clutching her limp hand in a tight, frantic grasp. Amelia was lying back on her satin pillows with her eyes closed, paying not the least attention to her father's muffled moans. The Prince's four sisters, subdued and miserable, clustered round him as he entered the room, clinging heavily to his arms and obviously looking to him for reassurance. Augusta exclaimed, 'George! We thought you were at Brighton. Oh, I am so glad you have come! Father says he wants to be quite alone with her. We are to go away. George, I think he is ill again. He is acting so strangely.'

He did his best to soothe them,

kissing each one upon the cheek and bidding them be calm, striving at the same time to control his own mounting despair. 'Where is Mama?' he inquired.

'At Bath,' supplied Mary. 'She went there a week ago to take the waters for her rheumatism. The Earl of Westmorland is on his way there now to fetch her.'

The Prince nodded, satisfied that all was being correctly ordered in this dire emergency, and said kindly, 'Go now, my darlings. I will see what I can do with Papa. Perhaps I can persuade him to let you come back in a little while.'

They whispered their thanks and tip-toed out of the room, casting backward, anguished glances at the still figure on the bed. Softly the Prince closed the door upon those strained, white faces and turning, approached the bed. The King did not look up, but Amelia opened her eyes, smiled at her brother and said wearily, 'What a fuss everyone is making of me, George. One would think I was at death's door, when all I have is a very stubborn cough and a slight fever.' She laughed, with some of her old gaiety. 'I had to make pretence to be asleep so that the girls would go away. I could not stand their gloomy faces. How I rejoiced when I heard your voice at the door.'

He swallowed hard, controlling himself with an effort. It would be cruel to let her see that he too was desperately worried about her, for she had often teased him in the past about his careless attitude towards life, saying, 'George, when you start to worry I know there is cause for alarm.'

Amelia's tired glance strayed towards the King. 'Papa is the one who merits your concern. I think he is ill again. He came in about an hour ago, tried to urge me to rise and go down to supper, and then fell to weeping, remaining as you see him now.'

'I'll send for the physicians directly,' he promised. He added with an attempt at lightness, 'You are his favourite child, my dear. You have but to cough and

Papa fears the worst.'

'I wish I did not feel so tired,' she complained. 'This cold has made me mighty weak I can tell you. Charles will chide me for catching cold again. He made me promise to take good care of myself when he was not by to protect me.'

'Charles?' he queried, momentarily at a loss.

'He is staying at his sister's house at Weybridge and presently recovering from an attack of bile.' Her eyes, bright with fever, looked suddenly anxious. 'I pray that he is in no danger from it.'

'Oh, yes, Fitzroy.' He had forgotten about Amelia's lover. Ten months previously Amelia had given notice to the Privy Council of her intention to marry, a fact which had, with difficulty, been kept from the King.

'Charles is my husband, George. Last October we were married at Upwey, that little village near Weymouth.'

Had he really heard aright? Was she delirious? No, her speech was lucid

149

enough. 'Who married you, dear?'

'Parson Selby of Upwey parish church.' She smiled reminiscently. 'We gave our names as Miss Warwick and Mr. Windsor. The poor man did not in the least suspect that we were not all we seemed.' Amelia began to cough, a racking paroxysm which went on and on, while he stood helplessly by, powerless to aid her. The King still clung to her hand. She tried to wrench it away, weakly irritable at this tiresome encumbrance, but that fat, pink monster was like a limpet crab and refused to be prised off.

Amelia fell back on her pillows, exhausted, still trapped by that implacable, persistent hand. 'George,' she whispered, 'will you try to arrange for Charles to come to me? I know it is selfish of me when he is ill too, but I need him so.'

Fervently he promised. 'I'll get him, my dear, do not you fret.'

She gave a long, shivering sigh and closed her eyes again. 'That will make me so very happy.'

He sat on the side of the bed, waiting for her to doze off before essaying the unpleasant business of arranging for the removal of the King. Suddenly her eyes snapped open. 'Were you not at Brighton, George? Why did you come home? Not on my account, I trust?'

'Oh, no,' he answered vaguely, relieved to be able to tell her the truth. 'Charlotte has been naughty.'

'Let her marry while she is young,' she murmured.

The inert figure sprawled across the bed, heaved suddenly into life. The King sprang to his feet, gesticulating wildly. 'No, no, none of my daughters shall marry! My sons have disgraced the Sacrament of marriage. I shall keep my daughters. All, all of them!'

The Prince tried to calm his father and succeeded in persuading him towards the door. Wrenching it open he pushed the King unceremoniously through and into the arms of a surprised footman. 'Take His Majesty to his apartments, John, and send for the physicians through one of my equerries,' he whispered urgently. Swiftly he returned to reassure his sister, but she had no need of his attentions. Amelia was dead.

★ ★ ★

After the death of his favourite daughter, the Princess Amelia, King George III, stricken with grief, lapsed into permanent insanity, thus necessitating the setting up of a Regency. Among Amelia's possessions were found three keepsake rings, in them a lock of her hair under a crystal set with diamonds. 'Amelia' and 'Remember me' were inscribed on the rings. Amelia had known very well that she had not long to live, but who were the intended recipients of the rings?

152

Part Two

THE NUNNERY

WARWICK HOUSE

1811

Princess Charlotte studied Mr. Beechey's new miniature of her, painted in profile, and made an extravagant grimace, pulling her mouth into comic, hideous distortion. 'I look like an actress,' she complained.

Miss Cornelia Knight, a small, dark bustling woman, the Princess's new lady-companion, successor to Lady de Clifford, clucked her disapproval. 'Mr. Beechey has caught an exact likeness of your features, Your Highness. You look pretty handsome and well you know it, you vain creature.'

'Too handsome for Young Frog?' asked Charlotte innocently, trying to draw Nottie out on the subject of the Dutch Prince whom her father was pressing her to marry. But Nottie would

155

not be drawn, nor would she pamper her charge's mischievous tendency to gossip. The Princess was too like her mother in this respect and any resemblance to that eccentric lady must be firmly eradicated.

Immediately after Miss Knight's appointment, which had followed upon the 'locked bedroom' episode at Blackheath, the Regent had given specific instructions that his daughter's high spirits were to be curbed whenever it seemed that they were leading her beyond the bounds of propriety. Miss Knight did her best, but it was not easy to alter the decrees of nature, to subdue the regrettable tomboyishness inherent in the Princess from birth, to transform the stable language into the language of a lady, to persuade Her Royal Highness against standing with her stomach thrust forward and her legs apart, to sit without showing an inordinate length of white frilled drawers, or indeed to do anything without an undignified lapse of decorum. Miss Knight, though she felt it was presumptuous of her, nurtured a sense of anxious pity for the gay, good-natured Charlotte, whom she had come to regard with deep affection. At sixteen most girls of good family enjoyed a constant round of balls and fêtes, looking for suitable husbands, and having a great deal of fun in the process. Apart from an occasional visit to the opera, permission for which had to be obtained before-hand from the Regent — with precisely one week's notice given — Charlotte rarely went abroad after six o'clock in the evening. Each day she was allowed to drive out in her carriage, round and round St. James's Park, chaperoned by two ladies, two outriders and a postilion. If, by chance, an acquaintance of the Princess was to drive by her carriage, her or she might not stop for conversation, and only if the Princess were to look directly at the person concerned were they permitted to bow an acknowledgement of her presence. In fact, the poor child's life was so circumscribed, so hemmed in by rules and regulations, that it was small wonder she suffered from persistent headahces and mysterious pains in her stomach, which came and went like the phases of the moon, or that her behaviour should frequently degenerate to the level of schoolgirlish pranks, at which exercise she was distressingly adept.

Ever since the establishment of the Regency the Princess had led an almost nun-like existence. As Regent, her father had unlimited power to order her way of life, a power hitherto restricted, not by compulsion, but rather by the adverse opinion the King had of his son's treatment of his wife and daughter. Now that opinion lay dormant in the mind of the old man who crept about the passages of Windsor, muttering to himself, sometimes darting into the Music Room to play upon the harpsichord and bring his tortured soul some ease. The Regent reigned supreme, King in fact, if not in name. His word was law. Therefore the Princess must endure, and endure was hardly too strong a word thought Miss Knight, for the Regent was a man of whims. Often he would give written permission for his daughter to receive a particular person at Warwick House, only to withdraw it at the last moment without stating a reason, valid or otherwise, for his change of heart. Miss Knight could not count the number of times Charlotte had sobbed out her frustration in her bedroom while she, Miss Knight, was faced with the daunting task of informing a lady or gentleman below that the Princess was not 'at home'.

Sometimes the Regent would send for Charlotte and lecture her for as much as an hour at a time upon any subject with which he was obsessed at the time, the Whigs, the Tories, Catholic Emancipation, his brother, Frederick, whose fall from grace over the selling of commissions in the Army had driven a wedge between himself and his elder brother — all were grist to the mill which ground out his indignation. Small wonder that Charlotte trembled with nervous apprehension every time she must cross the courtyard to Carlton House to answer a summons.

All this time, while Miss Knight's thoughts chased each other like playful puppies round and round her brain, Charlotte had been regarding her companion expectantly. Miss Knight dragged herself back from the realms of speculation and obliged by saying diplomatically, 'The Prince of Orange, whom by the way I do desire Your Highness not to refer to as Young Frog,' she shuddered delicately, — 'Such a *vulgar* name, applied by people of the most spiteful dispositions — is a very quiet, personable young man.'

'Personable!' Charlotte shrieked her derision, causing an expression of pained resignation to flit across Miss Knight's face. 'He is about as personable as my over-shoes. He is tall, thin as a pole, pale as a ghost and his breath smells of garlic. He reminds me of my cousin, Gloucester.'

This summation of the young man's appearance found Miss Knight looking aghast. 'But, my dear,' she expostulated, 'you are betrothed to him. Why did you agree to have him if you hold such a low opinion of his physical peculiarities?'

Charlotte pushed out her lower lip and toyed with the miniature, an interesting little conceit. Belonging to it were thirty or forty dresses done on isinglass which could be placed over the miniature, allowing the colour to be seen through. It was rather like dressing up a doll. Privately Miss Knight thought Charlotte too old for such foolishness.

Charlotte retracted her underlip and switched her mood with the facility of a chameleon changing colour. 'I have to get away from here, Nottie. You know I am little better than Papa's prisoner. I want an establishment of my own, and the protection of a husband, who will take me to balls, dance with me, make love to me, quarrel with me and placate me with the gift of a pretty bonnet.' She rose to her feet, pushing back her chair, and strode towards the window, a tall, well-built girl with the brilliant colouring of her mother, but with smaller, more sharply-defined features. She had had the good fortune not to inherit the long Guelph nose, nor the heavy-lipped mouth of her forbears and her eyes, unlike those of her father and grandfather, did not protrude when she became excited. Her face could not in any sense be called delicate, but her nose was straight, her mouth firm-lipped and her eyes set wide apart. Someone had once described her as healthy-looking, which was perhaps as apt a description as any of this flamboyant Princess. Underlying all this outward well-being, however, was a taut bundle of mixed emotions rapidly developing into various neuroses, which had been sparked off by the hatred between her father and mother, and the unpaternal hostility of the former. Miss Knight's heart went out to her as she stood, tapping her foot by the window, looking out at the curved driveway fronting Warwick House and the parade of elms, dripping diamonds of water from the recent spring rain.

'That is not a very good reason for taking a husband,' the companion argued gently, 'and you do not mention children as one of the blessings to be derived from marriage.'

Charlotte pulled a face. 'I do not much care for children,' she confessed with her usual frankness. She shrugged. 'Perhaps Frog is not so bad. He may improve upon further acquaintance. After all, I have only seen him once, at that ridiculous dinner-party Papa gave for us. Can you imagine, Nottie? The Old Begum, the four inmates of the harem, Father, Frog and myself, all sitting in the Gothic conservatory at that enormous table and discussing nothing more diverting than the Tsar of Russia's poor neglected wife, when all the time Napoleon Bonaparte is rampaging about Europe and threatening to annex England to his already vast Empire?'

'I think perhaps that particular

subject is best left alone,' stated Miss Knight wisely. 'I have no doubt that Your Highness would have expressed an admiration for the French Emperor which would have put His Highness into a rage, caused him to quarrel with you and forbid your visit to the theatre this coming Wednesday. You would have returned home in tears again I suppose.'

Charlotte pirouetted away from the window, admiring the flirt of her tiffany skirt. 'They say the Russian Emperor is very handsome. Papa says that all the ladies swoon when they see him for the first time.'

'How very inconvenient,' replied Miss Knight, smiling slightly, a comment which drew no response from Charlotte for her thoughts were once more on the wing. 'Of course, I could marry my cousin Gloucester,' she said, fetching up before a portrait of that gentleman, now in his thirty-fifth year and looking not at all like his painted image, which slyly flattered without blatantly deceiving.

Miss Knight came as near to snorting

as a lady of refinement could permit herself. 'The Duke of Gloucester is betrothed to your aunt Mary,' she reproved, 'of which fact you are well aware.'

'Ah, but he would rather have me,' came the swift retort. '*I* am the heiress-presumptive to the throne of England.'

'Why so you are,' rapped back Miss Knight, 'and behaving at this moment so like a spoiled child that I had quite forgot that particular circumstance.'

At this juncture a knock on the door prevented Charlotte from delivering her usual spirited response to Nottie's 'sarcastics'. 'Enter!' she called.

A female servant, holding a letter at some distance from her, as though she thought it might possibly be contagious, came in and curtseyed to Charlotte. 'What is it, Susan?' The Princess smiled with her usual good humour.

'A letter, Your Highness, from Carlton House, brought over just this minute by a footman.'

Charlotte flung a startled glance at Miss Knight, took the letter and nodded a dismissal to the waiting girl. When she had gone, closing the door softly behind her, Charlotte cracked the seal and unfolding the letter, began to read, her face tense with anxiety lest her father had discovered yet another of her 'sins' which required a personal reprimand. As she read, however, a look of genuine astonishment widened her eyes. 'Lord, Nottie, Papa is bringing the Prince of Orange over here within the hour. He says,' her eyes flew over the lines of bold handwriting to find the place — 'he says, 'in order that you may become better acquainted with he whom you will make the happiest man alive. The Prince is so eager for your company that I have not the heart to send him back to the Netherlands without first permitting him to make his adieu. I do not think you will have to suffer his absence for long, for he intends to inform the Stadtholder, his father, of the happy outcome of his visit here and to make all necessary arrangements for the wedding. The Queen tells me that she will see to the making of your trousseau . . . '

Slowly, Charlotte put aside the letter, and now there was more than anxiety in her blue eyes, there was fright and a hint of despair not commensurate with one of her tender years. Miss Knight thought she looked like nothing so much as a trapped animal which has given up hoping for anything more than a long, lingering death. 'He is in earnest then,' whispered Charlotte. 'Papa really does want me to marry the Prince of Orange.'

'Certainly he does, my dear child. Do you think he would have announced your betrothal to the whole world if he did not?'

'Oh, God!' Charlotte covered her mouth with her hand. Miss Knight sprang to her feet, her kind eyes lit with compassion. Advancing upon Charlotte she took her hand, looking up into her face searchingly. 'Dearest child, it is not too late to turn back.' She added worriedly, 'It will cause a fuss, no doubt, but I shall do all in my power to help you. I shall not let His Highness prevail upon you to . . .'

'No, no, Nottie.' Charlotte was laughing at her, with another of those lightning changes of mood. 'I have got the virgin frights today. He will do as well as any other I daresay, and I must get away. I must, or I shall run mad.' She squeezed Miss Knight's hand affectionately and kissed her cheek, saying reflectively, 'I remember Aunt Augusta telling me once that it is better to marry *anyone* rather than remain a prisoner all one's life. At least one has some status in the world.'

Her companion, though she did not venture to say so, thought this a very poor philosophy indeed. 'You had better change into your most charming gown, my dear,' she suggested quietly. 'The Prince and your father will be here directly and you want to look your best, do you not?'

'I do not!' declared Charlotte stoutly, greatly to Miss Knight's amazement. 'I shall wear my purple satin with the black lace trimming. If he sees me at my *very worst*, and looking a *perfect fright*, then he will never be disappointed in me.' Having delivered herself of this profundity, Charlotte galloped out of the room calling over her shoulder, 'Come and help me with my bridal vestments, Nottie, and remind me to write to Miss Elphinstone after our visitors have gone. As she is my very dearest friend she must know all my *feelings*.'

Miss Knight nodded, pondering grimly upon the fact that Miss Margaret Mercer Elphinstone was Charlotte's only friend, the only one at least with whom she was permitted to correspond. Please God, prayed Miss Knight, send her happiness.

★　★　★

The Regent was full of bonhomie, bubbling with enthusiasm and overflowing with *bons mots*, which mood of exuberance Miss Knight found to be rather exhausting, coming as it did after half an hour's battle with Charlotte over her *toilette*, during which time she had only just managed to persuade the Princess not to wear a diamond head-band stuck with black ostrich feathers. 'Your Highness will look like a walking hearse!' she had moaned, at which Charlotte had collapsed with laughter and prancing sedately round the room, lifting her feet in imitation of a horse, had sent Miss Knight into hysterics. To the companion's intense relief, however, Charlotte had at last conceded the point and had agreed to the substitution of a plain pearl band. She still looked like something out of a comic opera — Miss Knight's private opinion — but since she was adamant in her refusal to wear anything other than the purple satin, there was no more to be said. One might as well save one's breath.

The Regent was favouring Miss Knight with an expansive and knowing smile. 'You and I, Miss Knight,' he said, 'shall sit here in the drawing-room, warming our knees at the fire, while the young people whisper their secrets in the saloon. An hour together should make them pretty fair acquainted I think.'

The Prince of Orange, who was indeed tall, thin as a pole and pale as a ghost, exactly as the observant Charlotte had described him, said nervously, 'I trust, Miss Knight, that Her Highness is in good health today?'

Miss Knight bobbed a curtsey and answered that Her Highness was remarkably well and would be here upon the instant. Right on cue Charlotte swept into the room — Miss Knight suspected that the minx had been listening at the door — and performed an elaborate curtsey before her father and her prospective bridegroom. The former, after a single

171

startled glance at his daughter's attire, beamed, and the latter coughed timorously, gave a stiff little bow, and coughed again.

The Regent recovered from the undeniable shock of his daughter's appearance with commendable speed, kissed her on the cheek, took her by the hand and drew her towards her betrothed. 'Take her, sir,' he commanded the embarrassed young man, 'take her and *woo* her. Miss Knight and I shall remain here for just one hour, after which time you must bid each other farewell, I hope with the shedding of a tender tear.'

Charlotte and the Prince stood stockstill, staring at the Regent with a kind of unwilling comprehension until he gave them both a playful little push in the direction of the door. 'Into the saloon with you,' he said with heavy jocularity 'and do not you, Orange, presume upon my fatherly generosity and trust.' Privately the Regent thought the Prince looked devilish sickly, but such was his relief at having disposed of his troublesome daughter, that he would have married her to a Frenchman if such a dreadful personage would have obliged him by carrying her to the Continent and out of his life for ever. The Regent was now firmly fixed in his determination to obtain a divorce from his wife. Charlotte was, after all, only heiress-presumptive to the throne. He intended to beget an heir-apparent, and in the not-too-distant future.

Charlotte faced the Prince of Orange in the saloon and wished that she had dressed more becomingly. She suddenly felt very sorry for this young man who had been thrust upon her. They had, in fact, been thrust upon each other. He had feelings too. Perhaps he was not at all enchanted with the prospect of marrying her. She, selfish, vain creature — Nottie was right — had assumed that the doubts were all on her side. Having settled these thoughts in her mind Charlotte's warm, generous heart soft-ened towards the Prince and she bade him be seated, herself taking up a position directly facing him. She was particularly careful not to show her drawers. In her purple satin, straight-backed and demure, and with her feet tucked well back, she looked like a mature dowager. It was fortunate that there was in the room no pier glass to reflect Charlotte's image. She would undoubtedly have subsided into girlish giggles, causing her suitor yet further embarrassment. The Prince was discreetly coughing behind his hand. The high, snickering sound acted as an irritant on Charlotte's taut nerves. Making a conscious effort she suppressed what Miss Knight would call her 'impatient look' and said with the utmost sweetness, 'You are to return to the Netherlands then, sir?'

He coloured to his ear-tips. 'Much to my regret, Ma'am, I fear that is so.'

'Should we not call each other by our Christian names?' Charlotte suggested very boldly and could not resist adding, 'Since we are to be married I feel sure

Papa will give his permission for us to do so.' She conjured up a quick imaginary picture of William on their wedding night saying, 'If Your Highness will be pleased to assume the marital posture I shall endeavour to consummate our union.' The ridiculous notion prompted the beginnings of a smile which bubbled and effervesced into helpless laughter.

The Prince was looking perplexed. Lord, she was being awkward again. Determinedly Charlotte steadied herself and brought the conversation back to a normal, polite level. 'I am apprehensive at being alone with you, sir,' she admitted, appealing to what masculine instincts for chivalry he might possess. 'Pray take no notice if I behave oddly. We have known each other such a little time and are expected, I believe, to behave like lovers.'

He responded at once, smiling his relief, which she thought was a distinct improvement on his usual sombre demeanour. 'You are not more apprehensive than I . . . Charlotte.'

She said gaily, 'There, you have managed to say my name. Let us begin again then. What shall you do when you return home, William?'

'Why, rejoin my regiment I think, until the negotiations for our marriage are completed, and then I shall come over to England to claim you.'

'Shall you like living here in London?'

He answered with grave politeness, 'I do not think I shall be here long enough to find out.'

Her face matched his in its degree of solemnity. 'Of course, I suppose you will have to return to your regiment until this wretched war is over. Lord, I shall be left here all alone to pine for you, a sadly neglected bride, I fear. I do not find that prospect at all pleasing I assure you.'

Charlotte congratulated herself that she was behaving very well, making all the right responses, giving the impression that she was a weak, feeble creature who could not exist without the support of a man. His alert grey eyes, which were perhaps his best feature, contained an expression of polite puzzlement. 'You will be coming with me, will you not Charlotte?'

Charlotte pitied him. It was just like Papa not to have mentioned a little thing like the heiress to the throne being permanently domiciled in England. She explained, as tactfully as she could, the peculiarities of her position. 'I am the heiress-presumptive to the English throne, William. I may not leave England without Parliament's permission, which I think they will not give.'

He frowned. 'But you will be my wife, Charlotte. I too am my father's heir. One day I shall be Stadtholder of the Netherlands. Your place will be at my side.' He grew a little desperate, confused by the vehemence of her statement and the stubborn set of her mouth. 'I understood from His Highness, your father, that there would be a clause in the marriage contract to the effect that you will be resident in the Netherlands after your marriage.'

In the ensuing, horrific silence, she began fully to understand the depth of her father's perfidy. His insistence that she marry the Prince of Orange revealed to her in a sudden, blinding flash of insight, how much he disliked her, perhaps even feared her presence in England. She made a grim resolution to fight Papa every inch of the way, if necessary, for her rights, her inalienable rights. The first step in that fight would be to make Orange understand where he stood in the matter. Her voice took on a cool, authoritative note. 'If, as you say, Sir, there is such a clause in our marriage contract, about which I am sure you must be mistaken, then it must be struck out. When I am Queen of England, which, please God, will not be for many years, you will be Prince Consort. Our son, if we have one, will be the future King of England. I do not intend to give up any of my rights here, upon that I am resolved.'

'But . . . but,' he was going very red in the face again, 'your father — the Regent said that he had arranged all with his ministers . . . he . . . '

'Arranged? Arranged what?' she blurted, all control fast slipping away in the face of this dangerous threat to her position. 'Tell me, Sir, for I swear I shall never marry you unless my rights are confirmed and all is made clear in black and white.'

He was as agitated as she now, and rising from his chair perambulated in little circles before her. 'I was not supposed to tell you this, Charlotte. Your father thought you might become distraught and . . . '

'And he was damned right!' yelled Charlotte, thoroughly out of temper. 'I *am* distraught and shall be so until you tell me what you have devised between you to deprive me of my *rights*!'

Quickly he capitulated, deciding that he would as lief withstand a regiment of French lancers as face Charlotte of England in a tantrum. 'The Regent wishes to obtain a divorce from the Princess of Wales and marry again,' he said miserably.

Charlotte dissolved into tears. 'I will not leave England!' she sobbed. 'I will not. I shall write to the Prime Minister and tell him how ill I am being used. Questions will be asked in the House, I can tell you. There will be such a great fuss . . . oh, oh!' Emotion got the better of Charlotte as she let her tears flow unchecked.

★   ★   ★

Oblivious of the mounting tension in the saloon, the Regent stretched his legs before the fire, admiring his shapely calves, and wondering whether Miss Knight was at all susceptible to a well-turned ankle. Apparently she was not, for she did not spare his legs so much as a single glance. The Regent confessed to being a little disappointed. He was proud of his legs. They were magnificent. Moreover, he liked female admiration, a thing which he had been able to command from the cradle, and still commanded, though there was little desire in him now for more than platonic relationships. From the age of sixteen onwards, he had engaged in a wild round of sexual excesses which had left him, at the age of forty, withered and drained, and though he continued to take 'mistresses' they saw very little of his bed and a great deal more of his foot-stool, upon which he nursed his gout-crippled limbs.

Perhaps Miss Knight needed to experience the full and blinding effect of his charm and personality before she would respond. Eyeing the lady speculatively, he extracted from his waistcoat pocket a gold snuff-box with a coloured enamel inlay on the lid. With a practised flick of his thumb he snapped it open. Miss Knight recoiled as a gold bird popped up, perched on the rim of the box and emitted a perfect imitation of the nightingale's jug. Smiling, its owner took a pinch of Tribony's 'Prince's

Mixture' between forefinger and thumb, applied it to his left nostril, then to his right, and inhaled delicately. Far from being thrilled, Miss Knight was a little repelled by the elaborate ritual which must be performed in order to make one sneeze and to stain one's upper lip a light brown. However, she put a good face on it and ventured to express her admiration of such a pretty device.

'Presented to me, Miss Knight, by Madame de Stael,' the Regent informed her. 'A most formidable and unconventional lady, a blue-stocking no less. She told Lord Byron that he was a demon and had no right to make love to poor Caroline Lamb.'

Miss Knight blushed, gave a little gasp and touched her fingers to her lips. The Regent was satisfied. He had not succeeded in charming, but he had succeeded in shocking, which was almost as good. Graciously he inquired if she had read Miss Jane Austen's novel 'Sense and Sensibility'. Miss Knight regretted that she had not. 'But, my dear lady, you must,' he insisted. 'I have two copies of the novel over at Carlton House. One shall be sent over immediately upon my return. I confess that I find Miss Austen's writings far more entertaining than any which have sprung from the pen of my friend Scott, though I should never dare to say as much to his face.'

'Miss Austen lives in Hampshire, does she not, Sir?' asked Miss Knight, more to keep the conversation on a safe level than because she was interested in the work of a lady novelist. Miss Knight preferred men novelists on the whole. They seemed to have such a lot more experience of life. In answer to her question the Regent replied, 'In the village of Chawton, I believe. Do you not find it astonishing, Miss Knight, that the daughter of a country parson can be so knowledgeable about affairs of the heart between men and women?' He added thoughfully, 'Though I suppose the fact that she has brothers may have something to do with that.'

Miss Knight nodded sagely and decided that she had better become acquainted with Miss Austen's work after all.

Without waiting for her to reply the Regent sat back, expanding on his theme, sure of the respectful attention of his audience of one. 'As for Scott, I am afraid that his sense of history is dubious. In 'Kenilworth', for example, we have him quoting lines of Shakespeare at a time when the poet was but a child. His work is full of such anachronisms, and yet one must admit to the sheer genius of the man and his ability to conjure up such believable characters.'

Miss Knight, who had met and detested on sight the bumptious, hypocritical little Scotsman, did not presume to argue on this point. It was infinitely better to be bored by His Highness than to be on the receiving end of a stream of abuse and complaints, both of which conditions Miss Knight had patiently borne in her time. Was he getting fatter, or was it just that the pearl grey broadcloth he was wearing made him seem so?

'Which reminds me,' the Regent rattled on, 'of a most singular discovery made by the Dean of Westminster. Do you know of it?'

A polite negation from Miss Knight encouraged the Regent to proceed, though he would undoubtedly have done so without the least encouragement at all. 'There was discovered a coffin which the Dean suspected might contain the mortal remains of Charles Stuart, who, as you know, was executed, or should I say murdered, by his subjects?' He paused impressively, as if to emphasize his generosity towards the usurped Stuarts, then contined, with an air of pompous pride which made her want to laugh, 'I was present, Miss Knight, at the opening of that coffin and had the most unique experience of looking upon the face of a dead Stuart for the space of half a minute before it crumbled to dust before my eyes.'

'Most extraordinary, Your Highness,' she murmured, shuddering inwardly.

'Yes, indeed, and from an examination of the skeleton, Mr. Wilkins, my surgeon, gives it as his opinion that the axe cut into the King's neck just . . . here!' Rising from his chair the Regent placed a finger on the back of Miss Knight's neck, just below the third vertebra, sending a cold shiver down her spine. She had a fleeting desire to scream, but at this dramatic moment in their tête-à-tête the unmistakable sound of weeping reached their ears. The Regent stiffened, pulled up short in mid-sentence, and without vouchsafing another word on the subject of Charles Stuart, which had suddenly become the least interesting in the whole world, rushed out of the drawing-room, Miss Knight following hard on his heels. Across the intervening passage they hurtled, and bursting into the saloon were confronted by a distressing sight. Charlotte, doubled up in her chair as though in pain, was crying uncontrollably. The distracted Prince of Orange kneeling at her side, was trying to comfort her, with markedly little success. Charlotte turned a blotchy, tear-streaked face towards her father as he came into the room. 'I will not live abroad,' she blurted. 'I will not!'

'Now, now, my dear,' soothed the Regent, deliberately misconstruing the meaning of her words. 'I know you cannot bear to have the Prince torn from your side so soon after your betrothal, but he will be back quite soon, take my word for it.' Saying which, the Regent seized the bewildered Prince by the arm, dragged him to his feet and bundled him out of the room. The backward glance he cast at Charlotte was anything but paternal.

WARWICK HOUSE

1814

Napoleon Bonaparte was kicking his heels on the island of Elba, close to his native Corsica, having been driven out of his kingdom by a revived European coalition, whose armies invaded France on two sides and forced Paris to capitulate. The Emperor abdicated at Fontainebleau and was given sovereignty of the little Mediterranean island. Great were the rejoicings in Europe, hardly one of whose ruling houses had not suffered from the attentions of the 'Corporal'. In London, bonfires blazed and the Regent prepared to entertain a galaxy of foreign royals to a spectacular round of balls, banquets, levees, military displays and processions, interspersed with such intellectual pursuits as visits to the universities of Oxford and

Cambridge and a tour of the Royal Academy. It also provided a splendid opportunity for the Regent to show off the grandeur of his houses and palaces, strut about in his impressive wardrobe of military uniforms, and titillate the palates of his guests with the gourmet's delicacies prepared by his French chef, a pupil of the great Carême.

In March the advance guard of royals arrived, in the person of the Grand Duchess Catherine of Oldenburg, the sister of Alexander I, Tsar of Russia. She took an immediate and hearty dislike to her host and proved this by walking out half-way through a musical evening arranged in her honour, at the precise moment when the Regent, bow poised, was about to delight her ears with a rendition of Mozart's Sinfonia Concertante in E flat. The Grand Duchess was quickly followed to England by the Tsar himself and King Frederick of Prussia. In the latter's train came General Blücher, drunk as a lord and easily the darling of the crowd. Lesser royalty, including the Prince of Orange and Prince Leopold of Saxe-Coburg, the latter of whom could find lodgings only in a small, cramped room above a grocer's shop, came hard on the heels of the big guns, and soon all were embarked upon a wild round of festivities.

The Princess Charlotte, mewed up at Warwick House with only her ladies for company, viewed these junketings from afar with a jaundiced eye, commenting sourly to Nottie that one would have thought that one's betrothed would refuse invitations in which his future wife was not included. The Regent had cruelly excluded his daughter from all the celebrations in retaliation for her continuing refusal to allow the 'residence clause' to be inserted in the marriage contract. He still hoped to persuade her to accept it, but so far she had stood firm, insisting that after her marriage she would reside permanently in England. To the Regent, the whole object of the marriage would be defeated if Charlotte stayed in England, a permanent, festering thorn in his side. He had therefore decided to teach his daughter a lesson, in the hope that it would bring her to her senses.

Unknown to her father, however, Charlotte had in fact received the Grand Duchess Catherine, that lady having made a point of calling at Warwick House to leave her card. Charlotte, placed in the unhappy position of being unable to reciprocate, the Grand duchess had overcome this little nicety of etiquette by bowling up in her carriage one fine May morning and requesting an interview with the Princess. Miss Knight, flustered and doubtful, could not withstand the might of Russia, and Charlotte was left alone with the formidable lady for over an hour.

The Grand duchess, whose brother had viewed with a certain degree of alarm, the joining together of the Dutch and British navies, resultant on a marriage between Charlotte and the

Prince of Orange, had a little diplomatic probing to do. She therefore congratulated Charlotte on her betrothal and suggested that she must be living in a maze of joy. Charlotte, who was delighted at being in the presence of a woman from her own station in life, a rare enough occurrence for her, at once proceeded to open her heart. 'I suppose,' she began warily, 'one cannot hope for love before marriage, Ma'am?'

The Grand duchess elevated her plucked brows and fanned herself vigorously with an ivory and lace confection made by the famous Monsieur Le Clos for Marie Antoinette. The Grand duchess had travelled to France incognito during the troubled days of the Revolution and had 'picked up' the fan, along with a number of other valuable little trinkets, before the blood had scarce dried on the unfortunate queen's neck. The sight of the fan filled Charlotte with envy, as did her visitor's exquisitely cut pelisse of peach-coloured velvet trimmed with sable. As for her bonnet, well that could have sprung from no less a place than the salon of the Marquise de Rousseau in the Place Vendôme.

In her lightly-accented English the Grand duchess refuted Charlotte's tentative statement. 'Lord, child, were you the seventh daughter of a King, you might expect very little from an arranged match, but as heiress to the throne of England, I should have thought that, within the bounds of reason and prudence, the choice was yours, and that you might certainly think to love before you gave any Prince the honour of your hand in matrimony.'

Charlotte seized the opening afforded to her. 'I do not love the Prince of Orange, Ma'am,' she confided impulsively, 'and I think he loves me only for my position.'

The Grand duchess nodded sagely. 'That is not unlikely,' she agreed. 'I have heard it said that Orange is a very ambitious young man.'

Charlotte put on her sorrowful look.

'I am committed,' she wailed, with a dramatic emphasis which did not go unnoticed by the Grand duchess. The Princess, she decided, had a great deal of her father in her. She went on to argue, 'But the Archbishop of Canterbury has not yet made you and Orange man and wife, my child. There is time to withdraw if you find the marriage distasteful.'

'Withdraw, Ma'am!' Charlotte's eyes grew round, alight with a mixture of apprehension and excitement. 'I think my father would not like that.'

'Let him do otherwise then!' returned her visitor with a careless shrug. 'He will be angry at first, yes, but he will get over it. He is, after all, but a man underneath all those fine trappings.' She leaned forward, tapping Charlotte's knee with the coveted fan. 'I have heard, my dear, that he wears stays to contain all that excess flab.'

'Ma'am!' Charlotte was deliciously shocked. She started to giggle. The keen eyes of the Grand duchess were a-fire with mischief. Her light, tinkling laugh urged Charlotte on to further gusts of mirth. 'I see, my dear,' she went on, 'that your education has been sadly neglected. They have not instructed you in the art of female diplomacy which, I can assure you, is an accomplishment well worth acquiring. You must learn to outwit your father, whom, by the way, I find the most dreadful bore, and let him think you are doing his bidding, when all the time you are acting in direct contravention of his wishes.'

Charlotte was fascinated. Never before had anyone spoken to her like this, and to decry Papa so, when she had thought of him as little less than a wrathful god, who issued decrees and must ever be placated. It had never occurred to her that she might actually outwit Papa. She too leaned forward in her chair, making the Grand duchess wince as her knees parted and she clasped her hands together between her legs. 'What would you do, Ma'am, were you in my place? Pray tell me, for I should value your opinion very highly.'

The Grand duchess smiled, and thus invited, gave her opinion readily. 'That is simple, my dear. I should write to the Prince of Orange, a very diplomatic letter, expressing my deep regret at having changed my mind, and begging his forgiveness. Say, er — ' the Grand duchess made little circles in the air with her fan as if winding up her thoughts — 'Say that your position makes it impossible to marry anyone who is heir to a sovereign state, since your future husband's loyalties must be undividedly attached to England.'

'It is not only that I do not love him,' put in Charlotte swiftly, 'but Papa put a clause in the marriage contract providing that I shall live in the Netherlands.'

'The sly old devil!' exclaimed the Grand duchess, before she could stop herself. 'He wants you out of the way, my dear, depend upon it. Sovereign princes never do like their heirs, you know. To contemplate too long upon one's heir is, after all, rather like contemplating one's tomb. This is a fact which you must accept if you are to win your battles. Harden your heart against any little advances he may make to win your confidence and obtain your submission. Do you love your father?'

The abrupt question utterly confounded Charlotte. 'I — I do not know,' she faltered.

'Then you do not,' returned the Grand duchess emphatically. 'That is good. Accept that too and your conscience will be quiet when you use subterfuge to counter his attacks against you.'

The advice, couched in military terms, stiffened Charlotte's resolved to fight the good fight. If it had been proper to do so she would have gone down on her knees before the Grand duchess and kissed her hand.

After the exchange of a few more civilities, the Grand duchess had taken her leave, kissing Charlotte fondly and expressing a desire to see her again, promising to bring with her on the next occasion Prince Frederick William of Prussia — 'a very dashing young man, my dear, who will charm you out of your miseries.'

Charlotte's meeting with the Grand duchess had taken place in May. In June she wrote to the Prince of Orange, breaking off their engagement, having that very day deliberately picked a quarrel with him in order to arm herself with a plausible excuse — 'What has passed between us this morning makes it imperative that we should bring our betrothal to an end . . . ' The Prince, in a state of shock, took the letter to the Regent.

★ ★ ★

At five o'clock on a warm evening in July a strange procession passed through the portals of Carlton House, down the steps, and veering to the left, crossed the courtyard to Warwick House, passing en route two blank-faced sentries who guarded a small wooden gate set in the brick wall. This gate, a vulnerable point in the defences of Warwick House, led on to a narrow alleyway, at the end of which one emerged into the bustling activity of Charing Cross with its hackney-coach stand; the drivers belonging thereto, being accustomed to exchange pleasantries in rather loud voices, had provided Charlotte with a large part of the more dubious portion of her vocabulary.

From a window on the first floor of Warwick House, Miss Knight saw the file of people, like wary hunters, advancing upon the house, and running downstairs to the drawing-room, warned Charlotte that they were about to be boarded by a party of invaders. Her brother being a sea-captain, Miss Knight invariably 'went nautical', as Charlotte put it, when her habitual calm manner was disturbed by some startling event. Equanimity had treacherously deserted Miss Knight this evening. 'Your Highness!' she gasped. 'The Regent is on his way here. He has with him Lord Chancellor Eldon, the Bishop of Salisbury and four ladies!'

Charlotte went very pale. Her hand flew to her mouth. 'Oh, Nottie, what shall I do?'

Miss Knight straightened her lace cap, pulled back her thin shoulders and prepared to support and protect her Princess to the very limit of her endurance. But she might have been a fly on the wall for all the use she was to Charlotte when the Regent swept in with his entrourage, for she was summarily dismissed and instructed to show the strange ladies round the house. Having delivered his sinister command in a tone of voice calculated to quell the stoutest heart, the Regent actually slammed the door in Miss Knight's face. That poor lady could hardly believe him to be the same person who had chatted so cosily to her on the occasion of the visit of the Prince of Orange.

The shrinking Charlotte was now left to face her father and the other two men. She took up a defensive position behind the sofa, clinging to its curved back as though her life depended on it. Lord Eldon bowed courteously, but the Bishop of Salisbury, once her tutor, now her chaplain, nodded briefly, his shaggy brows drawn together in a tight little frown, his dark, close-set eyes accusing. Charlotte, who had known the Bishop since she was five years old, at which tender age she had taken a violent dislike to him, had christened him the 'Great U.P.' because of his peculiar manner of pronouncing the word 'bishop', making it sound like 'bish*up*'. Charlotte always had possessed the unerring ability to pin-point the single foible of speech or mannerism which would make a person look ridiculous, and having fastened upon this particular peculiarity very early in life, had goaded the Bishop into regarding her as his 'cross'.

The Regent launched into the attack without preamble. 'So, Miss, we do not wish to marry the Prince of Orange.'

These words were accompanied by a thunderous frown of disapproval. He went on, 'Do you understand the extent of the insult you have offered the House of Orange, all because of a stupid lovers' tiff? With your damned impertinent letter you may provoke an international incident which will have far-reaching repercussions, and consequences which you may live to regret.'

Charlotte answered spiritedly, 'I cannot insult myself by marrying a man I do not love.' Her bottom lip trembled. Fiercely she fought the desire to weep. She realized, too late, that she had given her father a splendid opportunity for verbal revenge. He took full advantage of it. 'I did not love your mother, Miss, but I married her because it was my duty to do so, and look at the result.' He pointed at her with a theatrically poised forefinger. 'I have an undutiful, ungrateful daughter.'

'Arrogant child!' boomed the Bishop, 'Ungrateful child!' in a sort of sonorous counterpoint to the Regent's song of hate. As usual, the Great U.P. succeeded in arousing in Charlotte a mixture of mirth and anger. What a pompous idot he was. And the others. Lord, look at them! Three grown men confronting her like great bullies at a public school! Only Lord Eldon had the decency to display the slightest sign of embarrassment at what he must have regarded as a most singular situation. Charlotte, fresh from the teachings of the Grand duchess Catherine, said clearly, 'My Lord Bishop, when I require an opinion from you as to my behaviour, I shall ask for it. Meanwhile, I am fixed in my determination not to marry the Prince of Orange.'

The Bishop's mouth opened and shut several times and even the Regent looked stunned. The latter recovered first and said with a dangerous glint in his eye, 'Well, I shall not waste my breath in trying to dissuade you from your purpose. Your household here will be broken up. Your ladies, including Miss Knight, for whom you seem to harbour a sickly sentimentality, better lavished on a pet dog, will be dismissed, and you will go to Cranbourne Lodge at Windsor where the Queen is now residing.'

Charlotte could not repress a cry of protest. 'But that is right in the heart of Windsor forest. No one ever goes there!'

The Regent revelled ignobly in his moment of triumph. 'Precisely, Miss. That is why I have chosen Cranbourne to be your residence. You will see no one, you will communicate with no one, not even your great friend Miss Elphinstone who is, I understand, presently residing here at Warwick House and doubtless encourages you in your reckless defiance of your father. You will be locked away from the world until you come to your senses.'

Charlotte wept, angered that her persecutors should see her so upset, yet unable to withhold the pressure of tears. Mercer Elphinstone had been her friend for five years, a willing confidante, the recipient of all her secrets. Charlotte had revealed things to Mercer, including the details of a certain amount of dangerous dalliance with Prince Frederick William of Prussia, which not even Nottie was privileged to hear. Now Mercer, but recently returned from a six months' visit to Paris, was to be torn from her. Perhaps she would never see her again.

'The Queen,' resumed her father, affecting not to notice his daughter's distress, 'will see to it that you are properly instructed in the ways of a dutiful daughter. Due largely to the influence of Her Majesty, my sisters have never behaved in the disgraceful fashion I have been pained to witness in you.'

'Ah, do you say so?' She would not let him get away with that. 'Aunt Gussie lives in sin; Aunt Sophie has a bastard at Weymouth; Aunt Amelia married without consent, a *commoner* and had a child by him; and Mary and Elizabeth are the greatest spreaders of gossip alive, because they have so little else to occupy their thoughts. They might not have behaved so badly had not the Queen been mighty free with her instructions to dutiful daughters!'

The Regent's face darkened to a dreadful purplish hue. Indeed the sight of his apoplectic countenance almost frightened Charlotte into thinking that she had gone too far and precipitated some sort of seizure. He roared at her, 'You are speaking of a great lady! You seem to forget that my mother is the Queen of England!'

'And you, Sir,' his daughter bawled back at him 'seem to forget that *my* mother is the Princess of Wales!'

Lord Eldon, hiding a smile behind a discreet handkerchief had to admit that 'Young Prinny', as Charlotte was known among the members of the House, had scored one there.

By this time the Princess was fleeing from the room. The Regent shouted after her, 'Come back, Miss. I have not done with you!' But she did not heed him, and with an exasperated sigh he let her go. He rubbed his hands together. Now for Miss Elphinstone. She could go about her business smartly and take Miss Cornelia Knight with her.

★　★　★

Charlotte raced upstairs to her bedroom, pushing aside her astonished maid, a dangerously exciting resolve taking shape in her mind. From her wardrobe she selected a bonnet and shawl and having flung them on, rummaged about in her satinwood dressing-table where she kept her ribbon money. From one of the drawers she took out a guinea piece which she judged to be sufficient for her purpose. Clutching her shawl tightly about her, Charlotte ran out of the bedroom, down the curving staircase and pausing momentarily on the bottom tread, one hand on the carved 'pineapple' of the newel post, was aware that an argument was raging in the drawing-room between her father and the Great

U.P. She caught a snippet of their conversation, first her father's loud, strident tones, ' — and if you had done your duty . . . would not have had a rebellious hoyden for a daughter . . . hold you responsible . . . ' answered by the Bishop's high whine, ' . . . never was a biddable child . . . remember the time she smothered my dinner with pepper . . . ' Lord Eldon's voice, moderately intervening, striking the single note of sanity, could occasionally be heard.

Charlotte left them to it and crossing the marbled hall floor, raced down the steps of Warwick House, across the courtyard and on towards the small guarded gate and the passage leading out to Charing Cross. The sentries, completely failing in their duty, watched her curiously and stepped respectfully back to allow her to pass, wooden-headedly convinced that their task was to keep people out rather than to keep people in, and not at all able to cope with this unlooked-for situation.

Casting a quick glance over her shoulder to ascertain whether or not she was pursued, Charlotte fled down the narrow lane and came out into Charing Cross. There were few people about, it being the supper hour, and it was with a great deal of relief that the Princess caught sight of a vacant hackney against which the driver, one Thomas Higgins, leant negligently, idly flicking his whip. Her approach, with the obvious intention of hiring him, sent Mr. Higgins leaping up on to the box with a shouted, 'Where to, Miss?'

Charlotte caught her breath, then managed to instruct Mr. Higgins in what she hoped was a very firm voice to take her to 'Connaught Place, if you please, in Connaught Square.' Then she was inside the hackney and pulling the little door to with a slam.

Excitement and the knowledge that she was embarking upon a great adventure, gradually took the place of terror in Charlotte's mind as, with a mounting sense of elation, she sat back against the musty leather cushions. A sharp, pungent smell inside the hackney teased her nostrils, a smell she was quite unable to identify. Never having been much in the vicinity of male servants, Charlotte did not recognize the odour of tobacco. She sniffed, and decided that the smell was not at all unpleasing. Months later, when she had her own establishment and that same smell became a part of her life, it would always remind her of her journey to Connaught Square and induce a quick flutter of terror in her breast. The driver had called her 'Miss'. Lord, how delicious! Just wait until she told Nottie. And then she remembered that Nottie was to be dismissed, and that this was the reason for her hasty flight to her mother's town house. Feelings of joyful anticipation quickly disappeared, to be replaced by the onset of gloom and the certainty that if she could not persuade her mother to help her, she would be locked away in the country until she died from sheer boredom.

The hackney jogged on, through the square, up past the royal mews and along Cockspur Street. The evening was fine and sunny. Charlotte, peering out of the small, dirty window between the soiled leather curtains, envied the couples walking together in the park, free as air. Some had dogs on leads, old married people those; others were holding hands and looking into each other's eyes, laughing, happy. Charlotte thought that it must be a very fine experience indeed to be happy. What did it *feel* like to be so?

Mr. Higgins brought his horse to a halt with a loud 'Whoa!' considering himself fortunate to have picked up the fair young lady in the yellow bonnet, who gave him four times the correct fare and ran off without waiting for change. A lady-companion to the Princess of Wales, he reckoned, out for a tryst and keen to get back before she was discovered. Stone me! A guinea! That would buy a few pints of Barclay's best, and a highclass whore from the stews.

Whistling up his horse, Mr. Higgins drove off.

The footman who opened the door of Connaught Place froze with horror as he recognized the illustrious visitor. Everyone in the household knew that the Princess of Wales and her daughter were forbidden to see one another without permission from the Regent. Charlotte cut short the young man's confused courtesies and demanded to see her mother. When informed that the Princess of Wales was out driving with Lady Charlotte Lindsay she declared her intention of waiting and was shown into the drawing-room where, though it was high summer, a huge fire blazed in the hearth. Charlotte smiled as she remembered how often her mother complained of 'zis foul Eenglish vether'. She was beginning to feel very hungry. On a sudden impulse she rang the bell and ordered dinner from a pop-eyed maidservant.

★ ★ ★

Within the next hour a series of scrawled messages issued from Connaught Place, borne by running footmen. Ill-spelled, some almost unintelligible, they winged their way to the houses of the great in London. Having refreshed herself with cold veal and salad the Princess had applied herself with frantic assiduity to the composition of these missives in which she summoned those whom she thought might be of use to her in this present crisis. The result of her labours was that a number of hastily called-up carriages and hackney coaches were now on their way to Connaught Square containing curious, agitated, alarmed or impassive occupants, according to the temperaments of the recipients of those grubby pieces of paper.

First to arrive was the Duke of York who roundly chided his niece for being a naughty, troublesome child, kissed her on both cheeks, wept over her and called his brother a damned scoundrel for using her so. The dukes of

Sussex and Cambridge, the Earl of Liverpool, Mr. Henry Brougham — the latter a lawyer and strong partisan and upholder of the rights of the Princess of Wales, — the Princess Sophia, the Princess of Wales and Lady Charlotte Lindsay arrived at Connaught Place in that order.

Caroline smothered her daughter in a cushiony, maternal embrace, and upon learning the reason for her precipitate flight from Warwick House, muttered, 'Zat *canaille*, ve vill see him laid in ze dust, nein?' thus assuring Charlotte that, so far as her mother was concerned, everything would be done to help her. Everyone sat round in the drawing-room drinking liberally, sampling Caroline's famous claret, some for the first time, and complimenting Her Highness on her excellent taste. Gradually there developed a kind of carnival atmosphere, as the subject of Charlotte's rebellion against her father, and her reason for it, was bandied back and forth, chewed over, swallowed, digested, regurgitated and swallowed all over again.

Henry Brougham, that aspiring politician, with his sharp, questing nose, gave it as his opinion that the Princess Charlotte could not in any way be forced to marry the Prince of Orange if her inclination was against the match, and that as to the question of her residence, it was unthinkable that the heiress to the throne should be allowed to go out of England. Had everyone forgotten how the King had prevented the Prince of Wales from taking part in the campaign against Napoleon? The Duke of York was forced to muffle a laugh at this. He was thinking of George, arrayed in one of his pretty uniforms, snugfitting over his stays, and leading a charge against Napoleon's infantry. Even if George had the stomach for such an exercise it was doubtful if he would have sufficient skill with a sabre to prevent his being decapitated during the first charge.

A footman came in to announce that

Miss Cornelia Knight was below. 'Send her up!' trilled Charlotte, who, seated bolt upright on her mother's sofa, was really beginning to enjoy herself. Surrounded by all these supporters she felt invulnerable, armoured against anything her father might try to do to her. Miss Knight was duly shown up, appearing out of breath and flustered. Leaping from her seat, Charlotte embraced her companion and led her to the sofa, forcing upon her a glass of claret. Nottie was dismayed by her charge's apparent disregard for the seriousness of her situation. Could the silly child not see that she had worsened an already bad state of affairs by running away? The Duke of Sussex, he of the imprudent marriage, shared this point of view, and took it upon himself to admonish his niece, since everyone else seemed to think that she had accomplished something vastly clever. 'I think you should go back to Warwick House at once, Charlotte,' he said sternly. 'You will achieve very little by such foolish behaviour, and although I admit that you have certain cause for complaint, this is not the way to remedy your situation.'

Charlotte's face fell. She liked her Uncle Sussex, who was the kindest, most gentle of men, and lacked the bullying, rather brash manners of his brothers. She was, however, in no mood to be thwarted. She looked round the circle of faces. 'You *will* help me?' she pleaded. Having listened to Sussex, however, they all appeared a trifle hesitant. No one responded to Charlotte's appeal. Was the barometer of opinion turning against her? Still no one spoke and in desperation Charlotte turned to her mother. 'Please, let me stay here with you, Mama. I cannot go back there. He wants me to go to Windsor and live with the Queen. I hate that old woman! I hate her!' She began to sob violently. 'Oh, God, I *detest* her!'

Several faces expressed shock, even Caroline's, though her reaction was occasioned not so much by the indiscretion of her daughter's outburst, but by the fact that she was secretly determined to leave England at the earliest possible opportunity. She too had been ignored during the peace celebrations in London, and for her it had been the final, the spirit-breaking humiliation. She would not remain any longer in a land whose ruler hated and despised her so. She remembered how she had sat, hour after hour, dressed in a formal gown of blue velvet, her diamond tiara nestling amidst the absurdity of an orange wig, waiting to receive the foreign dignitaries who never called. Not even Frederick William of Prussia, for whose cause her father had died fighting, had deigned to present himself at her door, for fear of displeasing the Regent. She knew they all thought her slightly mad and perhaps, in a spirit of defiance directed against their unceasing hostility, she had given colour to that idea, behaving oddly, entertaining social outcasts such as Shelley and

Byron at her dinner-table, hinting at non-existent lovers, because there was nothing else, save eccentricity, with which she could fight them. And now here was her daughter, begging for sanctuary and a refuge, which she had no power or even desire to give.

Henry Brougham, who knew of Caroline's intention, intervened to say, 'Your Highness, you know very well that all here have your best interests at heart. Although your action in coming here was perhaps a little ill-timed,' — Brougham flinched at the look of accusation in Charlotte's eyes, but pressed on hurriedly — 'it has achieved something, in that it has drawn our attention to your difficulties. I would therefore suggest that a paper be drawn up for all here to sign, to the effect that you do not wish to marry the Prince of Orange, and that any future marriage you may make will require an under-standing that you shall remain in England.' He waved an airy hand, 'An Act of Parliament if you like.'

Relieved nods of assent greeted this diplomatic face-saver and Charlotte, out-numbered, out-talked, out-man-œuvred, tearfully agreed that she would return to Warwick House. At once York and Brougham got down to the business of thrashing out the wording of the document, while Charlotte engaged in desultory conversation with her Aunt Sophia, that lady remarking that once she had made a bid for freedom and had failed lamentably to achieve her purpose. 'I hope, my dear, that you are more fortunate,' she observed.

* * *

It was breaking dawn before the document was worded to the satisfaction of the Duke of York, who insisted that Brougham draw it up in 'lawyer's jargon'. Charlotte, all her shining happiness of a few hours before dissipated in the welter of talk which had subsequently taken place, stood by the huge bow-window watching the slow, creeping greyness of the sky change into pink and gold and glowing orange. His task done, Brougham came to stand beside her. She bent upon him reproachful eyes, red-rimmed from lack of sleep and the shedding of tears of disappointment. 'I did not think,' she said, 'that you would refuse to stand by me.'

His thin, intelligent face bore an expression of tender sympathy. 'Your Royal Highness,' he protested kindly, 'I assure you that quite the contrary is the case. As to your marriage, you must follow your own inclination entirely, but your returning home is absolutely necessary.' He pointed down at the square below them, fast materializing into distinguishable shapes as the sun mounted the heavens. 'Today, Your Highness,' he reminded her, 'there is to be an election. In a few hours' time all the streets and the park, will be thronged with people. I have only to take you to this window and show you to the multitude and tell them your grievances, and they will rise on your behalf.'

'And so they should,' came the spirited rejoinder, 'for I have great cause for grievance.'

Brougham smiled at her indulgently and went on, 'The commotion would be excessive. Carlton House would be attacked, perhaps burned down; the militia would have to be called out; blood would be shed; and were Your Royal Highness to live for a hundred years, it never would be forgotten that your running away from your father's house was the cause of the mischief, and you may depend upon it, such is the English people's horror of bloodshed that you never would be forgiven.'

Charlotte looked stricken. 'Well, Sir,' she said quietly, 'if you are right, I have no other course but to return to my bondage.' He lowered his eyes, for he could not meet that clear, candid gaze, nor answer the pathetic words of surrender.

It was broad daylight as the hackney

coach containing Charlotte and Miss Knight drew up in the courtyard before Carlton House. The Regent, having been informed by his brother York of all that had passed at Connaught Place, kept his daughter waiting for half an hour before consenting to receive her, and then it was only to repeat his command that she should go at once to Cranbourne Lodge. Miss Knight was ordered to go to Warwick House, pack her belongings and leave the following morning. Charlotte's adventure, her brief taste of freedom, was over. Whether she had achieved anything at all remained depressingly in doubt.

* * *

The frigate 'Jason' rode at anchor off the English coast, about half a mile out from South Lancing. A jolly boat, crewed by six sailors, had just been lowered from the port side and was making for the shore at a spanking pace, bringing the captain of the frigate to meet and escort the important passenger who waited on the beach to be rowed out to the ship.

The passenger, dressed in a pelisse of dark green velvet, with a dashing hussar hat of black beaver set jauntily on top of a stiffly curled wig, sat on the breakwater idly scanning the horizon. Beside her slouched a young man of some fourteen years, who seemed sadly out of countenance at the prospect of crossing the English Channel on a day when the wind was rapidly freshening to produce a heavy swell on the grey, swirling mass of the sea.

William Austin, about whose person fierce controversy had raged some eight years previously, son of a docker and adopted by the Princess of Wales when he was a few months old, turned to his 'mother' for reassurance. 'I do hope, Mama, that I shall not be sick. I should find that most disaggreable.'

Caroline studied the pale moon face of her adopted son and reflected that, unprepossessing as he was, he was the only person who had given her any real affection during her long, unhappy stay in England. He had been, it was true, a most objectionable child. How Sheridan had hated him! How affronted Byron had been when Willikin had wetted on his pearl-grey pantaloons, how distrait they all were when Willikin had clung to her and called her Mama and she had mischievously answered, '*My sweet Prince!*'

Willikin had grown into rather a dull young man, too listless to have an opinion upon anything more important than the fall of a cravat, or the possibility of a particular horse winning the St. Leger. But she loved him. He was, when all was said and done, the sum total of her achievement in England, all she had to show for twenty years of ridicule and ostracism. 'If you feel sick, Villy,' she advised practically, 'Hang your head over ze side of ze sheep and give your breakfast to ze fishes. Ze journey vill not be long, and your malaise vill pass.'

'I suppose so,' he agreed doubtfully, then, struck by a sudden thought, 'Shall I like it in Italy, Mama?'

There was amusement and a certain amount of sly cynicism in her reply, 'Oh, yes. You vill like it. It is vere all ze outcasts go. Ve shall meet a great variety of exiles, poets, painters, halfpay colonels. Ve shall meet zem all zere, Villy.'

William, quite oblivious to her heavy sarcasm, asked anxiously, 'You will find me a suitable wife in Italy, will you not, Mama? One with a handsome fortune. I do not wish to remain a pauper all my life.'

She retorted sharply, 'I sink you do very vell for one who had so poor a start in life, Villy.' He had the grace to blush. Mama had never before spoken to him in quite that tone of voice.

The sailors were beaching the jolly boat. Caroline signalled to two ladies sitting further up the beach, the only members of her household who had elected to come with her, more because they had nowhere else to go than because they felt any great loyalty towards her. The women rose and walked down to the boat. The baggage having been rowed out to the 'Jason' the night before, there was nothing for the sailors to see to save their human cargo. The Captain came towards Caroline and bowed. 'You are ready, Ma'am?'

'Yes, I am ready. I haf been ready for twenty years, Captain.' He smiled, a foolish, embarrassed smile, and offered her his arm. An unexpected sound broke the silence on that deserted beach. Caroline whirled round and looked back towards the shore. A small crowd had gathered along the footpath leading to the beach. A few people were waving handkerchiefs, and a ragged cheer went up, repeated over and over again. Caroline started to weep. She did not know why.

CRANBOURNE LODGE

1815

In February, 1815 Napoleon escaped from the island of Elba and the Hundred Days began, culminating in Wellington's glorious victory at Waterloo. While the famous squares formed, withstood, died bloodily, repulsing countless charges by the French cavalry; while Wellington, mounted on Copenhagen, took refuge within the nearest square of British infantry whenever the French came forward to the bayonets; while commanders acted at cross-purposes, messages miscarried, casualties mounted, and Napoleon endured the agony of piles, the Princess Charlotte remained mewed up at Cranbourne Lodge in the middle of Windsor forest, her only companions the Queen and her aunts Mary and

Sophia, the two latter having been dragooned into sentry-duty by their mother.

The Queen had assured her daughters that when Charlotte went for the summer to Weymouth, Augusta and Elizabeth would accompany her, leaving them free to return to their London houses and an existence hardly less humdrum than that which they had left behind them at Cranbourne Lodge, save that they would have the satisfaction of doing nothing without being subjected to the constant surveillance of their mother.

Now indeed was Charlotte a prisoner, her days carefully regulated so that every minute was usefully employed. Each afternoon, sitting at her embroidery, at which craft she was remarkably unskilled, the Princess must listen to her grandmother relating incidents which had taken place in the early days of her marriage to the King. Any reference to His Majesty was put into the past tense — 'The King was very liberal in his religious views, being of the opinion that Quakers are the most dedicated people on earth; the King was always very fond of music; the King was very skilled at making buttons.' It soon became clear to Charlotte that, as far as her grandmother was concerned, the King was dead. She found it hard to keep from groaning aloud as the Queen related, for the thousandth time, the details of her Coronation, and of how she had met the Duke of Newcastle coming out of a small chamber adjacent to St. George's Chapel in Westminster Abbey. The chamber had been converted into a powder-room and was to be reserved exclusively for the use of the Queen. 'How confused he was when he saw me! He had not anticipated my arrival at the Abbey for at least another quarter of an hour. I made pretence not to notice anything, but I can tell you I did not much relish using my commode after that!'

Often the Queen would break off in the middle of one of her reminiscences to rebuke Charlotte with such remarks as: 'Charlotte, is it your intention to insult me? You know you may not yawn or cough in the presence of the Queen. It is a rule of the Court which the King was particularly concerned should never be broken.' And so it went on, until Charlotte began to think that it was preferable to be mad, like her grandfather, and totally oblivious to one's surroundings.

Two days before Charlotte was to go to Weymouth to pass the summer, a visitor arrived at Cranbourne Lodge. Thomas FitzClarence of the Queen's Own Hussars, son of William, Duke of Clarence by his liaison with Mrs. Dorothy Jordan, came to pay his respects to the Queen before taking up an appointment as aide-de-camp to the Duke of Wellington. After luncheon, he suggested that Charlotte might care to ride with him in the park, 'to work up an appetite for the next go at the trough'. The Queen shuddered at her nephew's coarseness of speech, but having no good reason to refuse the request, and not wanting young Fitz to gossip about the situation at Cranbourne, gave her consent to the proposed expedition, but with the stipulation that the two young people did not go beyond the dairy farm. This being agreed upon, the horses were sent for and Charlotte, who could not believe her good fortune, galloped towards the farm as though the devil were after her. She did not draw rein until she got to the Queen's Ride, where she dismounted and flung herself on the ground beneath the shade of a huge, spreading elm.

FitzClarence was close behind her and presently joined her under the tree. He was a tall, handsome young man, very like his mother, with curling brown hair, distant grey eyes and a crooked mouth which made him look as though he found life a perpetual source of amusement. Charlotte had always liked him. Though she had seen little of him recently, he had always been a part of her childhood. 'Dam'me, Charlotte,'

Fitz laughed, stretching out his long lanky frame beside her, 'if you ain't in a devilish hurry. Where's the fire?'

Charlotte raised her arms above her head, her mouth gaping in a prolonged yawn. 'Oh, Fitz,' she sighed. 'You have saved my reason by coming here today. I wish you could stay with me forever and be my knight in armour, protecting me from all those who seek to harm me.'

His homely, honest face expressed mild concern. 'I heard ye were in trouble, Charlotte. Orange wasn't it?'

'Ye-e-s,' She lay back, dragging out the word on another easing yawn. 'It's a long story.'

He cushioned his head against a clump of grass. 'I learned most of the details from Father,' he told her, 'who had it from Uncle York.' He waited expectantly, eager to hear her side of the business, but she did not want to talk about the harrowing saga of misunderstandings which had led up to her present sorry state, so she asked, 'How is your mother, Fitz?'

'Pretty fair, thank'ee, Charlotte,' he answered amiably. 'In debt up to her ears, as usual.'

Charlotte made a sharp little sound of disgust. 'Uncle William treated her shabbily, casting her off like that. Ten children she gave him, and he repaid her after twenty years by abandoning her. He gives her a pension, I suppose?'

'Four hundred a year,' confirmed her cousin.

'Not much to show for all those years of fidelity, is it? Lord, Fitz, what a family spawned us.'

Fitz rose spiritedly to the defence of his sire. 'Papa has always been good to me, you know.'

Wisely Charlotte did not pursue the matter, but she did wonder briefly whether it might not be better to have been born a bastard. Those born on the wrong side of the blanket always seemed to command more affection than their legitimate brethren. Suddenly she turned towards her cousin, propping herself up on one elbow to look at

234

him. 'Fitz,' she pleaded, 'ask Uncle William to talk to Papa about me. He might be able to persuade Papa to let me out of this horrible prison.'

He hesitated, staring at her pale, desperate face. There was something he could tell her which might lighten her heart, but he dared not, because he wasn't quite sure of his facts, and Charlotte looked so miserable that it would be cruel to raise her hopes for no reason. After a brief struggle with his conscience Fitz decided to remain silent. He said only, 'I'll do my best for you, Charlotte.'

'Yes, yes, I know you will.' But her voice lacked conviction. Fitz began to feel really sorry for her. She was damned pretty was Charlotte. He wondered why he had not noticed it before. With his usual frankness he said what was on his mind. 'Dam'me if you ain't mighty handsome, Charlotte. Any fellow would be lucky to get you.'

She found that rather amusing and began to laugh, but the laugh caught in her throat and turned into a sob. Poor old Fitz. All he had wanted was a pleasant canter through the park and some diverting conversation, and here she was blubbing all over him. Angrily she wiped her eyes, managing another weak laugh. 'Thank you for your pretty compliment, Fitz, but it is of little use for me to look well when there is no one here to appreciate it.'

'*I* appreciate it,' he assured her.

'Do you, Fitz?'

Their heads were very close together, chins almost touching eyes locked. It was she who leaned forward for the kiss. Dazedly Fitz obliged. All at once, Charlotte, love-starved and burning, had her arms about his neck and was smothering his face with kisses, nipping at his nose with her teeth, caressing his ears and the nape of his neck, instinct alone telling her how to please and arouse desire. Fitz was taken completely by surprise, the more so because she succeeded almost immediately in 'touching him up', as Fitz

236

himself would have expressed it, making his response as unrestrained as her attack.

Breathing heavily, his mind confused and temporarily devoid of rational thought, he pushed her over on to her back and started to fumble with the neck of her bodice. She did not resist, though the buttons on his tunic bit through the flimsy stuff of her gown to cause her considerable discomfort and pain. Her exposed breasts aroused him even further. Lord, he had not thought her so well endowed! He buried his hot face in the soft mounds of flesh and heard her gently moan. Devil take it, she'd done for him! He rolled off, panting, his heart thudding and his face pouring sweat. She lay with her eyes closed murmuring 'Fitz, darling Fitz.' He was calming down quickly now and mighty glad that he had not made a fool of himself. She would have let him, no doubt about that. To lessen her disappointment he decided to tell her all that he knew about a certain matter, and to hell with the consequences. 'Charlotte,' he began, still puffing from his exertions, 'Papa told me that the Regent has written to Coburg and invited Prince Leopold to come over to England in the New Year. I think he means to offer you in marriage.'

These words, acting upon her like a douche of cold water, had the effect of making her sit bolt upright. 'Leopold of Coburg!' she exclaimed. 'I saw him once or twice during the peace celebrations. He was out riding in St. James's Park and would have presented himself had not the outriders whipped up my carriage horses.' She looked very pensive and added, 'He is very handsome.'

Fitz grinned. 'As to that, I am no very good judge, but I hope he will bring your troubles to an end, Charlotte.'

'So do I, oh so do I, Fitz,' she breathed. Without embarrassment she adjusted her dress, eyeing him with solemn approval. 'I would have let you, Fitz.'

'I know,' he said, 'and ain't I damned glad ye rushed me, Charlotte. Ye deserve something better than a bastard for a lover.'

THE PAVILION, BRIGHTON

1816

Charlotte, waking to a cold, grey February dawn and the sound of Mr. Nash's workmen building the new Banqueting Hall, felt a tremendous sense of well-being, a supreme experience, which she savoured to the full as she lay on her back, indolently putting off the moment when she must get out of bed and expose her body to the chill morning air. She was nineteen years old, and in three months' time she would be married to Leopold. Beautiful, wonderful Leopold, of the dark, curling hair and the large, soft brown eyes.

Summoning up all her determination, Charlotte pushed back the covers, flung on a velvet night-wrapper and jumping down from the high bed, ran to the

240

window. In the distance, beyond the gardens, the narrow street of fishermen's houses, and the bow-fronted window of Cowley's bun shop, she could see the pale yellow sand glistening with frost, and the sea, green and turbulent, tossing up clouds of spume which rose and sank and was sucked back into the rolling mass, only to be tossed up again as the breakers tumbled in. Charlotte never tired of watching this endless repetition, the ebb and flow of the tide and the ever-changing sky colouring the water in different hues. In the weeks before Leopold came she had formed the habit of sitting by the window for long minutes at a time, surveying the timeless ritual until her head ached and her eyelids drooped with weariness. But not today. Today, after breakfast, she would go out in the pony-chaise with Leopold and Mercer, the latter now reinstated, and drive along those golden sands until it was time to turn about and come back to drink chocolate in the Rotunda with the

Regent and the Queen, both turned unaccountably benign, sitting opposite to her and Leopold and nurturing true love with the radiance of their smiles.

It was perhaps fortunate for Charlotte's peace of mind that she did not know the reason for her father's volte-face, for the Regent, having committed his daughter to purdah, had received certain reports from Italy to the effect that his wife was conducting herself indiscreetly with one Bartolomeo Pergami, a soldier in the army of Napoleon's brother-in-law, Joachim Murat, and that there were those who would give evidence of adultery in a court of law, in the event of the Regent instituting divorce proceedings. Elated by this intelligence, the Regent had felt he could afford to be generous to his daughter and allow her to marry young Leopold of Coburg, who had already evinced an interest in her by writing to the Duke of York. York, who had a great deal of sympathy for Charlotte, had advised his brother that this was as good a match as any for Charlotte, and that the Regent had a duty to see that the Hanoverian line did not die out, the legitimate line that is, he had added with his wry sense of humour, for there really was no need to worry about the opposite sort — they were flourishing like the green bay tree.

The Regent had told his brother, somewhat brusquely, that he had not the least intention of doing so, as York would very soon discover, but he took the point and invited Leopold to come to England to meet Charlotte. After a dreary few months at Weymouth, spent in the company of her aunts, Charlotte had arrived at the Pavilion, the venue chosen by the Regent for her meeting with Leopold, just before Christmas, not without some trepidation. But she need not have worried. All seemed to have been forgiven and forgotten and she was welcomed by the Regent with his usual superficial good humour. The Queen too, relaxed her eternal vigilance and treated Charlotte less like a naughty child and more like a young lady on the threshold of womanhood.

Vividly Charlotte recalled her first meeting with Leopold. She had been so excited that she had hardly been able to stand still. The momentous interview had taken place in the Yellow Drawing-Room, with its water-lily gasoliers and huge wall paintings of Chinese landscapes, and Leopold must cover fifty feet of carpet in his journey towards her, the cynosure of all eyes, the envy of not a few male hearts.

Leopold had not looked at all nervous as he bowed before her, an immaculate figure in grey pantaloons and a frock-coat of blue broadcloth. She remembered with great clarity the perfection of his white stock, adorned with a gold, pearl-headed pin. He had looked directly at her, his eyes grave and considering, and she had felt her colour come and go as she imagined that firm, strong mouth clinging to hers and those beautiful, long-fingered hands caressing her. For the first time in her life

Charlotte had been struck dumb, had allowed her hand to be kissed, had listened to the conventional courtesies falling from the lips of a gentleman in trance-like silence. Later, fortified with several glasses of champagne, she had become more relaxed and had laughed with Leopold over the extravagant antics of the Landgrave of Hesse-Homburg, who had come to pay court to her Aunt Elizabeth, and was at that moment staying at the Pavilion. 'He must spend a week with the Queen first,' Charlotte had explained to Leopold, 'before he may go to Windsor to see my aunt. Poor Aunt Elizabeth, she will be forty-six this year. A miracle apart, I do not think there is the slightest chance of issue, do you, sir?' This opinion being accompanied by a giggle into her handkerchief, Charlotte had not noticed the look of disapproval directed at her, nor the slight tightening of Leopold's perfect mouth. She had chattered on, convinced that he found her as desirable as she found him, and had wished only that her marriage day was not so far distant in time.

Charlotte gave an ecstatic little sigh, yawned and stretched and thought it time to ring for her maid. At that moment a movement in the gardens below caught her eye. A woman was walking across the lawn towards the small house almost concealed by a grove of lime trees. The woman, dressed in a brown pelisse and wearing a pale yellow poke bonnet, walked with the aid of a stick, looking neither to right nor left as though she were in a hurry to reach the shelter of the house. It was early for anyone to be abroad, and Charlotte was curious. The woman was well-dressed, a person of quality without doubt. Suddenly she turned and called to a little dog trotting along at some distance behind her. Charlotte caught her breath. She had not seen Mrs. Fitzherbert since her last visit to the Pavilion in 1807. In those nine years she had become an old woman!

★ ★ ★

After the morning ritual of taking chocolate, Leopold and Charlotte walked in the gardens, unchaperoned, her arm linked loosely in his, a circumstance which recalled to her the strolling lovers she had seen on that memorable July evening when she had taken the hackney to her mother's house. How far away those troubled days seemed now. Charlotte wondered briefly where her mother was, but even Caroline existed in her mind only as a dream-figure, someone who had flitted through her life leaving little impression, gradually fading into the background and giving way to her present brilliantly-coloured world. For the first time in her life she knew what it was to be utterly content.

Leopold's thoughts, on the other hand, were far less complacent. He was wondering how to begin his little campaign of 'moulding Charlotte', a campaign he had determined upon directly after he had been introduced to his bride-to-be and had judged her an awkward, ungainly creature, though not at all bad-looking, and by all accounts a kind, good-natured girl. Leopold was not, at this juncture, stricken by Cupid's dart, though had he but known it, the God of Love had set the trap and he, like many another before him, was about to fall victim to the strength of Charlotte's personality. Those who give freely of love are bound, in the end, to receive it and Charlotte gave in abundance. There was a goodly harvest waiting to be reaped. For the moment, however, the trap had not yet been sprung and Leopold decided that it was time for his campaign to begin. The occasions upon which he saw Charlotte alone were few and far between and three months would pass before they became man and wife. He smiled at Charlotte, to take the sting out of his words, and ventured, 'My dear, I should prefer it if you would not laugh quite so loudly at the witticisms of other people.

When Lord Canning mentioned the matter of Lady Dudley's bonnet becoming wedged in her carriage window — you remember the incident at dinner last night'? She nodded wordlessly and he felt encouraged to conclude, 'You emitted sounds, my dear, which can only be described as — er, coarse.'

Charlotte looked slightly taken aback but gave no sign that she was offended by the rebuke. 'I remember,' she confirmed quietly. 'You whispered to me 'Doucement, ma chere, doucement,' and I must confess to being puzzled at the time. Now, however, I perceive your meaning. It has become a habit with me to laugh loudly.'

'I know,' he countered patiently, 'and I wish you would not, my dear.'

'If it displeases you, Leopold, then of course I will not. In future I shall laugh 'doucement', so that you will scarce be able to hear me at all.'

He smiled his satisfaction, charmed in spite of himself by her graceful submission. It was a good beginning.

'There is too the matter of your stance.'

'My stance?' Charlotte's eyebrows rose. She fought down a desire to laugh — loudly. Leopold was so serious. He was now regarding her with a severe little frown knitting his brows. 'You tend to stand with your stomach jutting forward and your legs, er, your legs . . . apart,' he finished bravely. 'This does not look very elegant, my dear. If you do not believe me, stand so before your mirror, when I think you will be immediately aware of the distressing effect resultant on such a stance.'

She was regarding him with a half-smile on her face. 'I do hope, my dear,' she said, 'that you are not going to bully me. I should find that most disagreeable. I know I have a great many faults. My dear Miss Knight, whom you have yet to meet, would agree whole-heartedly with you in your desire to improve me. You must discuss the matter with her and decide between you what is to be done with me.'

He met her frank gaze, bemused by

the mild reception of his criticisms. He had expected protests, sullenness, even a few tears. She really was rather handsome, with her lovely complexion and her fair, curling hair. One day she would be Queen of England and, God willing, the mother of a brood of fine, strapping sons. His sons. A sudden and most unexpected wave of tenderness swept over Leopold. He laid his free hand on the gloved hand resting on his arm. 'Do you know, Charlotte, I think we shall suit each other very well,' he remarked happily. Her smile was brilliant. 'I have not the least doubt of it, my dear.'

Charlotte congratulated herself that she had handled Leopold splendidly. Lord, what a pompous old darling he was! She would have to take him in hand. She would be so tactful that he, her dear 'Monsieur Doucement', would not even guess he was being manipulated.

★   ★   ★

The Crimson Saloon at Carlton House, lit by six chandeliers, presented a magnificent and pleasing spectacle. Charlotte, dressed in a gown of silver tissue trimmed with Brussels point lace, with a simply-designed chaplet of rosebuds, fashioned out of diamonds, on her head, stood beside Leopold before the improvised altar and pledged her vows of eternal fidelity. The solemn ceremony played upon her ever-fluctuating emotions and made her tearful at a time when she felt she had reached the very peak of happiness. To add to the slight feeling of depression which encompassed her, she could hear behind her the steady, insistent weeping of her father, who, like his father, invariably 'gave way' when a female member of his family became the central figure of some ceremonial occasion, be it wedding, confirmation, or merely a birthday anniversary.

After the conclusion of the ceremony, as the champagne began to flow, and congratulations were showered upon her, Charlotte's spirits began to revive. Her Aunt Mary kissed her cheek. 'Dearest Charlotte,' she said in her light, high-pitched voice, 'you have found happiness at last and will be presenting us, your aunts, with a fine nephew in no time at all, I think.'

Charlotte bubbled with laugher. 'Such an occurrence has been known to follow upon the celebration of a marriage, Aunt Mary.' She went on gaily, 'And in two months' time you too will be a bride.'

'A rather elderly one I am afraid,' replied Mary, and tried not to look in the direction of the Gentlemen's Social Table, where her future husband was making free application to a bottle of Madeira. Charlotte prattled on. 'It is not too late for you to . . . ' She stopped in confusion and stared intently into her glass of champagne, her cheeks uncomfortably hot. Mary was laughing at her. 'My dear, I was forty last month. I should not care to embark upon so perilous an enterprise at my time of life.'

Charlotte wondered how her aunt could avoid such an enterprise if fickle nature decreed otherwise. She hoped sincerely that Mary would not bear a child. It would certainly kill her at her advanced age. She said: 'You and my cousin Gloucester are almost the same age, I believe.'

'Yes,' sighed Mary. 'I was born in the year 1777 and he the year before. 1776 was the year when we were at war with the American colonies and they issued their Declaration of Independence. How long ago it all seems. When I was ten I can remember your Papa telling me that *he* could remember sitting on our Uncle Cumberland's knee and listening to him recount tales of the battle of Culloden.'

'The '45,' said Charlotte, pulling a face. 'The Great U.P. told me that those who fought for Charles Stuart deserved their bloody fate.'

'We all get what we deserve I suppose,' commented Mary cryptically.

Charlotte asked curiously, 'Why have

you not married Cousin Gloucester before, Aunt? You have been betrothed for five years. It seems a long time to wait.'

Mary stared at the young girl who had all her life ahead of her. Twenty years or more stretched before her in which to bear children. She could not keep a note of bitterness from creeping into her voice as she replied, 'The inclination for marriage lessens as one grows older. When I was your age, my dear, I was impatient, eager for life to open up and show me all its mysteries, the delights which I felt sure were lying in store for me, but it was not to be. Papa did not want any of us to get married.'

'How cruel,' sympathized Charlotte, who had known her grandfather, before he lapsed into insanity, only as a vague, fussy little man who patted her head and bade her be a good girl. Occasionally he had popped a sweet into her mouth.

'Oh Papa was not *cruel*.' Mary's

faded blue eyes held a look of faint indignation. 'He was always very gentle with us. It was just that he could not bear to part with us.'

'But he let Aunt Lottie go,' Charlotte reminded her.

'Yes.' Mary smiled reminiscently, 'and regretted it ever afterwards, especially when Napoleon made an alliance with her husband and gave him the title of King of Würtemberg. I remember that Royal wrote to Mama and addressed her as 'My dear Sister'. Mama was furious and wrote back to 'The Duchess of Würtemberg'. Your Papa had to intercept her letters and re-address them.'

Charlotte laughed heartily. 'And now it looks as if Aunt Elizabeth will be going abroad, if the Landgrave of Hesse-Homburg prospers in his suit.'

Mary bit her lip. 'I do not know who has the worst bargain, Elizabeth or I.'

'Aunt Mary!'

Charlotte was genuinely shocked. She stared at the stout figure before her, made yet stouter by a gown of pink velvet. Charlotte thought her aunt looked like a huge pin-cushion. 'Do you not love Cousin William?' she asked.

'Love? At my age? He will use me ill. I know it. But he will also set me free from my eternal perambulations after Mama, and I shall have a marital establishment of my own.'

'I suppose I have been very fortunate,' Charlotte said humbly.

'You have indeed, my dear,' returned her aunt. '*You* were born heiress to the throne.'

CLAREMONT

1817

Sir Thomas Lawrence studied his model with amused exasperation and wished that he could capture in paint that strange, elusive quality of expectancy which personified her, and gave one the impression that she was always upon the point of drawing one into some joyful and exciting conspiracy. He put down his brush, flexed his fingers, and appealed to her good nature. 'If Your Highness would but keep your head in a fixed position for as long as *one minute*, I could perhaps get something on to my canvas which would be a recognizable likeness.

She threw back her head and laughed, placing both hands on her bulging abdomen. Good Lord, if only he could 'freeze' that on to his canvas! It would make him more famous than da Vinci; she was a modern Mona Lisa revelling in her *grossesse*. That dark blue velvet suited her very well, and the chaplet of flowers, a form of head-dress she had favoured ever since her marriage day, made her look like a Grecian goddess. She had the proportions for one, a fine, strong bone structure, heavy-breasted and heavy-hipped, a Raphael goddess. He wished he could have the opportunity of painting her in the nude. But he could not paint commoners in the nude, let alone princesses. What was acceptable from George Romney was not to be tolerated from Sir Thomas Lawrence, painter to His Royal Highness Prince George, Regent. Even Romney hadn't got away with it. After studying in Italy for several years he had returned to England to produce a host of unclothed beauties which he had hoped to exhibit at the Royal Academy. As a member of the Selection Committee it had been Sir Thomas's unpleasant duty to reject the marvellous array of nudes submitted by his very dear friend. George had never forgiven him, or the Academy. Neither did Sir Thomas think he would ever forgive himself.

Charlotte was tilting her head slightly backwards and to one side, straightening her shoulders and letting her arms hang loosely at her sides. 'Like this?' she queried, cutting across his musings.

'Yes, yes,' he responded eagerly. 'Just like that, Your Highness. If you could but hold the pose for five minutes.'

She teased him a little. 'You are upping your price, Tom. You said just now, for as long as one minute,' then relenting because she liked him and because he had been a very good friend to her mother, she promised to 'stand fast for the next half hour, like the squares at Waterloo.'

He begged leave to doubt this extravagant claim, but thanked her none the less, and fell swiftly to work, executing great sweeping strokes of yellow ochre upon the canvas.

'Can I talk?'

'Certainly, provided that you move only your lips.'

'My throat might wobble.'

'Indeed it might, Your Highness.'

'Shall you show my belly?'

'Your Highness!'

'Oh, Tom, *Sir Tom*, do not profess to be shocked, for I know very well you are not.' She added slyly, 'Or is it that Papa having made a knight of you, you are going to become most dreadfully stuffy?'

He could not help laughing. 'Your Highness is being deliberately perverse this morning I think.'

'I am always perverse, Tom. At any rate my husband tells me so.'

He had known that she would get on to the subject of the adored one before long. The Prince was hardly ever out of her thoughts it seemed. Sir Thomas obligingly gave her the opening she required. 'His Highness is well this morning I trust?'

'Indeed, yes,' she answered promptly.

'He has gone botanizing.'

Sir Thomas shuddered. It was not his idea of enjoyable recreation to go crawling about on one's hands and knees looking for rare specimens of plant life. 'A very interesting hobby, Your Highness,' he observed. How brilliantly blue her eyes looked this morning. She was much too perceptive for him. 'Which you, Sir, would consider the most boring thing on earth to do.' He ducked his head to hide a smile, shielded by his canvas, not bothering to deny her confident assertion. He should have known better than to fob her off with an inane platitude.

Charlotte went on to talk of her husband and the simplicity of their daily life together. Walking, riding on horseback and in the carriage, occasional shooting parties, though neither was keen on the wholesale slaughter of wild life, visits to friends and relatives, were all discussed, dissected and remarked upon, Charlotte confiding that she enjoyed most of all the musical evenings when she and Leopold would sing together at the pianoforté before retiring to bed. 'It is so very strange,' she told the painter, 'Before my marriage I longed for gaiety, to be able to attend balls and parties and to make visits to the theatre. Now I am content with very little and I swear we do not go to the opera more than once in two months. I no longer have the least desire for the gay life.'

Sir Thomas opened a fresh pot of crimson lake and mixed it with the yellow ochre already on his wooden palette. From his breeches pocket he extracted a pair of square-rimmed spectacles which he stuck on the end of his nose. Over the top of the spectacles precisely calculating eyes carefully assessed the line of Charlotte's chin. He said wisely, 'Mundane activities can become like gala occasions when we perform them in the company of those whom we love.'

'Yes, that is very true,' she agreed warmly. 'Do you think I shall make a good mother, Tom?'

Her question took him by surprise. Royalty were not very often preoccupied with their potential aptitude for parenthood. He answered with perfect candour, 'I think any infant would be exceedingly fortunate to have Your Highness for a mother.'

'I shall not be much of a one for discipline,' she confessed.

His eyes kindled. 'That is exactly what I meant, Your Highness.'

She stifled a yawn. Posing made her tired, especially with this heavy weight under her heart. 'I shall require you to paint my child on each birthday,' she announced, 'and all my subsequent children on their birthdays. I mean to have at least six children. That is the absolute limit, you know. The Queen had too many in my opinion, with the result that she was quite unable to control them.'

Sir Thomas judiciously refrained from commenting upon the last and most frank part of Charlotte's remarks and contented himself with proclaiming that he would be pleased to paint all of Her Highness's children, should he live to see them.

'Oh, but you must continue to live,' she laughed, 'for I daresay I shall want you to paint my grandchildren!' She chattered on, asking after his family and about the new house he was having built at Hampstead. 'I suppose Papa keeps you pretty busy?' He nodded and gave vent to a very long sigh. 'The Regent gives me more commissions than I can easily carry out. He has lately commissioned portraits of all the great generals who were at Waterloo, and intends to build a Waterloo Chamber at Windsor to accommodate them.'

'Papa is a great builder,' admitted Charlotte. 'Shall you do all the paintings yourself?'

He roared with laughter. 'Your Highness, it is a task quite beyond the capacity of one man. I shall leave the artists in my studio to paint all the bodies, and I shall merely do the heads.'

This statement vastly intrigued her. 'Then I think you should give merit where it is due and write 'Body by so-and-so' on each canvas, right beneath your signature.'

This succeeded in throwing him into convulsions of laughter. He threw aside his brush. 'I think that is enough for today,' he said. 'Your Highness has shown remarkable self-control and I shall therefore release you on the instant.'

'If only to stop my chatter,' she finished slyly.

When Prince Leopold came in from his botanizing, he found his wife and Sir Thomas Lawrence both doubled up with mirth He joined in, not knowing the cause of their merriment, but simply because he felt so very happy.

*　*　*

On an evening in late October, Charlotte sat in her bedroom writing to her friend Mercer Elphinstone. Outside,

266

the leaves of the oaks were beginning to assume their autumn colours, and the birds flew back and forth in great agitation, darting from tree to tree, busy with some mysterious, indefinable preparations for the onset of winter. It was getting dark. Soon it would be time for the candles to be lit and the ringing of the supper-bell. Charlotte looked down at her swelling stomach. She was enormous, gigantic, a horrible travesty of her normal self. She could no longer bear to look at herself in a full-length mirror. The sight of that huge, permanent protuberance irritated her. She had the absurd notion that she would like to take a dagger and burst the swollen balloon of flesh. The baby was due now. Perhaps it would come tonight, creeping up on her in the small hours when she least expected it. Mrs. Griffiths, the mid-wife, had said that she was sure Charlotte would be delivered of a ten-pound baby, and because she was 'all out in the front', it would undoubtedly be a boy.

Charlotte propped her chin on her free hand. Lord, how tired she felt. Dr. Richard Croft, the accoucheur, was subjecting her to a starvation diet and twice-daily bleeding, a course of treatment which seemed to sap all her energy. She had talked to Dr. Stockmar, Leopold's physician, about the frequent bleedings, and he had stated, with a certain degree of caution, that they did seem excessive. On the other hand, Dr. Stockmar could not presume to interfere with such an experienced practitioner as Dr. Croft, whose knowledge of such cases was known to be vast. Stockmar was being diplomatic. Privately he was highly critical of Dr. Croft's drastic ministrations, but dared not say so lest he run the risk of being called a 'damned interfering foreigner'. He could therefore do little other than advise Charlotte to submit to the advice of the accoucheur and pray that all would be well.

Charlotte dipped her pen into the

new purple ink which she had purchased from Bartholomew's on her last visit to Windsor. It had a pleasing effect upon the cream notepaper embossed with her coat-of-arms. She had fallen prey to an unaccountable fit of despondency which she had endeavoured, without success, to shake off all day. It persisted, and she put it down to the fact that she was past her time. She wrote steadily for the next fifteen minutes, watched by a solemn-eyed spaniel who rested his chin on her feet, setting down sentiments which she could hardly believe expressed her true feelings. Carefully she read over what she had written:

'Claremont October 30 1817. My dearest Mercer,
I am glad that you cannot see your miserable friend at this particular moment, for she is a woeful spectacle to behold. I swear, dearest girl, that I have twins in my belly. There is not a gown large enough to

269

contain me. Pray God I shall be delivered soon, for I am already a week past my time. They say a woman in child-bed is very close to death. I feel so, and yet I do not fear it. Would it not be a marvellous thing to have one's burdens taken from one, to have the soul go free and unfettered, like a butterfly emerging from a chrysalis? As Shakespeare has it — 'It seems to me most strange that men should fear; seeing that death, a necessary end, will come when it will come.' No, I should not mind. Indeed, I should welcome it, for I think I am not destined for true happiness in this world . . . '

Almost she tore the letter up, but decided that Mercer was the one person in the whole world who could dispel her black humour with a brisk, encouraging letter, accompanied by the latest copy of 'La Belle Assemblée', from which she could choose a brand new wardrobe after her baby was born. This reflection reminded her that she had done very little in the matter of her baby's trousseau. Only after the repeated urgings of Mrs. Griffiths had she summoned up enough energy to send to London for three linen and three silk smocks, two shawls and an entirely impractical lace bonnet. Mrs. Griffiths had declared herself not wholly satisfied with these acquisitions, but as she had said, with the merest hint of disapproval, 'At least Your Highness's *son* will not go about *naked*.'

Charlotte smiled at the remembrance of the midwife's good, honest, worried face looking up at her from a disadvantage of six inches. She would bestir herself in the matter immediately after the baby was born — if it ever did make its appearance. Charlotte sighed, folded her letter, and placed it in an envelope, another recent innovation from Bartholomew's. Sealing the flap with red wax, she embossed it with her seal. The sound of someone calling her name had the immediate effect of lifting her low spirits. The spaniel's dreaming eyes widened, and his head came up. Charlotte bent down to stroke the silky red coat. 'Come up then, Penda,' she commanded. 'He wants us.' Jumping up from her chair, she ran to meet Leopold, the spaniel close at her heels.

★ ★ ★

Charlotte and Leopold were returning from distributing Bibles to the poor in nearby Esher village. Charlotte sat back in the phaeton, her knees protected from the cold by a fur rug, her hands enclosed in a beaver muff, while Leopold touched up the mare and sent her speeding homewards at a brisk trot. The sharp November wind had reddened Charlotte's cheeks which, framed by the fur-trimmed hood of her blue pelisse, presented a very charming picture indeed. Leopold evidently thought so, for every now and then he would glance at her, a smile parting his lips, a look of tender solicitude in his eyes. He had fallen deeply in love with his gawky princess.

Charlotte, catching one of his love-stricken looks, said cheerfully, 'I do not know how much benefit Mrs. Blundell will obtain from our gift. She can neither read nor write.'

'I suppose she may persuade her son to read to her, my dear. He has received a certain amount of schooling I suppose.'

Charlotte giggled. 'If he can spare the time from getting the village girls pregnant and turn his thoughts to more uplifting matters.'

Leopold smiled in spite of himself. At one time he would have frowned at her remark and offered a stern rebuke. He had long since discarded his plan to improve her, however, and had given himself up whole-heartedly to the whims of this joyful creature whom he had had the good fortune to marry.

'I am not at all sure about Dan Blundell's familiarity with the written word,' Charlotte was saying.

Her husband tut-tutted. 'Really, my dear, do not you think it rather ridiculous for us to give Bibles to the village people when so few of them can read?'

Smiling, she agreed that it was, and went on, 'I think we should try and start a school in the village, and employ the services of some competent woman to teach the children their letters. It is our duty as lords of the manor to do so.'

'Very mediaeval, my dear,' he replied solemnly. 'I take it you have no objection to my asserting the *droit de seigneur* and trying to match the prowess of the redoubtable Dan Blundell?'

She threw back her head and laughed in the way Sir Thomas had so admired. 'Oh, Leopold. You are so deliciously droll, my dear.'

They bumped along in companionable silence for a while, Charlotte wondering what Claremont would be like under a blanket of snow. She hoped very much that they would have snow this year. Last year there had been a light fall which had quickly turned to grey sludge, not at all diverting. She must write to Aunt Sophie this evening to thank her for a most elegant basket-work baby-carriage, lined with pink quilted silk, which she had sent down from Windsor, and to Aunt Mary, for the baby-walker of polished oak. Was it kind, she wondered, to put a child inside that wooden ring and allow it to propel itself all over the place in such a cumbersome contraption? How typical of Aunt Mary to be practical, and of Aunt Sophie to indulge in such a flight of fancy as to imagine that one would continually push a baby around on wheels! Perhaps she could harness her dog to the baby-carriage and let him run alongside her phaeton. The idea was mirth-provoking. Charlotte giggled. 'Ooooh!' She doubled over as a violent cramping pain gripped her abdomen and took her breath away. But in the midst of her discomfort she felt an overwhelming sense of relief. Only a few more hours to wait and she would be flat again. Quite gaily she called, 'Dearest, I think it is time. The child is coming.'

Leopold took one look at her, hand on stomach, face contorted by the prolonged contraction, and would have whipped up the mare had she not prevented him with a breathless, 'No, no, my darling! That will only make matters more uncomfortable for me. The baby will not be here for a while yet. He is but taking the precaution of leaving his card.'

In the face of his wife's stout-hearted appraisal of her situation, Leopold tried to remain calm, but the last few hundred yards to the door of Claremont House seemed like ten miles. With great care he helped Charlotte from the phaeton and up the steps of the colonnaded portico. The maidservant on duty in the hall understood immediately what was happening, and sped off to spread the alarm. Taking advantage of the brief moment before a score of willing hands besieged her, Charlotte turned to Leopold and took his hands in hers. 'Dearest heart, in a few hours' time I hope to give you a son. I want you to know that whatever the pain, however long the travail, I shall rejoice every minute, knowing that I have the love of so good and kind a man.'

Leopold did not believe it proper for a man to shed tears. Nevertheless, several trickled down his cheeks as he said thickly, 'If you want me, tell Stockmar, and I shall come at once. I shall not leave the house until you are safely delivered.' Then he kissed her full on the mouth, a lover's kiss which did not excite, but yet was more meaningful than any they had ever exchanged before. It was Charlotte who found the strength to pull away first. Slowly she removed her pelisse and hung it over a Chinese lacquered screen given to her by her father, and which had once adorned the Music Room in the Pavilion. On top of the pelisse she placed her muff. 'Leave these things here,' she said, 'and when I come down I shall put them on again, and you will take me driving in the phaeton to show the villagers our child. We two came into the house. We *three* shall go out again.' The conceit pleased her and she smiled brilliantly.

He nodded wordlessly and taking her arm went with her up the wide, curving staircase and on into her bedroom where he handed her over to the waiting Dr. Croft and Mrs. Griffiths. He stood uncertainly, reluctant to leave, until Charlotte gave him a little push, accompanied by one of her *outré* remarks: 'Go to your study, Leopold and read your books. You have done all that is required of you in this matter. Now it is *my* turn.'

Both Dr. Croft and Mrs. Griffiths found this highly amusing and in the face of their laughter, Leopold retreated with a repetition of his promise to stay in the house.

★ ★ ★

Charlotte, helped by Mrs. Griffiths, was undressed and put to bed while Dr. Croft retired to fetch his omnipresent lancet and bleeding-cup.

'I shall not bawl or scream,' the Princess assured Mrs. Griffiths as the midwife fussed with her pillows. 'It will only make Leopold feel bad if I do.'

This noble vow made Mrs. Griffiths snort with disdain. 'Serve him right,' she retorted. 'It does 'em good to hear the results of their attentions.'

There followed forty-five hours of protracted labour for Charlotte, during which time she was faintly intrigued to see Mrs. Griffiths disappear and re-appear several times with a change of dress. Charlotte commented upon this singular circumstance and was told by the good lady that it was always her practice to do this during the labour of one of her patients, to keep up the lady's spirits and divert her from the more painful part of the procedure. And indeed, Charlotte did find it diverting to watch the comings and goings of the midwife, who invited her opinion upon each transformation. One gown in particular was admired very much by the Princess. It was of dark blue velvet decorated at bodice and wrists with lace ruffles and worn under a silver-mesh spencer. She stated her preference and Mrs. Griffiths smiled. 'This dress,' she declared, holding out the skirt, 'is seventeen years old. The last occasion on which I wore it for professional purposes was when Her Royal Highness the Princess Sophia was delivered of her son at Weymouth.'

'You were there?' asked Charlotte in surprise. 'I do not remember. I was only four at the time.' She added thoughtfully, 'I remember the Punch and Judy show though.'

'Her Majesty would trust no one else,' boasted Mrs. Griffiths proudly. And then, as though her integrity were in question, 'Of course, I have renovated the gown since then, to bring it up to the latest fashion.'

Charlotte smiled at this. 'Fashions

come and go, Mrs. Griffiths. That low-waisted style will come in again, you may depend upon it.'

Mrs. Griffiths had spoken of Sophia's 'trouble' without the slightest embarrassment, for it was well-known that the Princess now visited her son openly at Weymouth, the old man at Windsor not being in a position to forbid her, and the Queen too old and ill to care whether she did or no. Having Charlotte at her mercy, so to speak, and extremely vulnerable in her present state, Mrs. Griffiths ventured to satisfy her curiosity upon a particular point, a nagging doubt which had haunted her for years. She said, with an assumption of indifference which did not go unremarked by Charlotte, 'Is it not a pity, Your Highness, that the Princess could not marry the gentleman she loved?'

'Yes, a great pity,' agreed Charlotte.

'A gentleman of birth and breeding, I have no doubt.'

'Yes.' Charlotte's eyes were wary. 'General Garth is very well connected, I believe, and now Mrs. Griffiths, I am suddenly very hungry. Dr. Croft will permit me to partake of some bread and butter — I daresay.'

'Yes, Madam, of course.' Mrs. Griffiths curtseyed and retired, concealing her disappointment. It was plain that Her Highness had no intention of disclosing the name of the real father of the Princess Sophia's child. Surely she did not think that anyone had been taken in by that nonsense about General Garth?

Dr. Croft bled his patient six times during her labour and after the first plate of bread and butter, denied her the solace of more. The consequence of this was that when Charlotte finally pushed into the world an eleven-pound, still-born male child, she was upon the point of utter physical collapse. She lay back on her pillows, white-faced and shallow-breathed and stretched out her hand to her husband, who had been summoned immediately after the birth. 'I am sorry, my dearest,' she apologized.

The lump in his throat seemed to grow and grow as he stared down into those dark-circled blue eyes. For her sake he forced it down and answered briskly, 'Nonsense, my dear. A little mishap. There will be others. Why, you are not yet twenty-two.' The corners of her drooping mouth lifted. 'The eighth Henry said very much the same thing to Anne Boleyn when she presented him with a daughter.' Smiling weakly she squeezed his hand.

'Well, of course,' he replied, with a brave attempt at jocularity, 'if you should presume to fail me again, I shall have no recourse but to chop off your head.'

'Darling Monsieur Doucement,' she murmured. 'Forsaking all others, keep thee only unto me ... ' Her voice trailed off and she fell into a fitful sleep.

★　★　★

Mrs. Griffiths prepared the gruel for her patient with painstaking care. How

283

could the Almighty be so cruel towards one who had already suffered so much in her young life? Mrs. Griffiths knew all about the Regent's harsh treatment of his daughter before her marriage. She had served the Royal family for too many years to be ignorant of any of their doings. Word always reached her, whether she was in London, attending upon some great lady; in the country, helping a member of her own family; or at Windsor itself, aiding one of the maidservants to birth the progeny of a footman, or even of the Duke of Cumberland. She had delivered five little bastards in as many months for him. Not only was Mrs. Griffiths excellent at her job, but she had a very still tongue, an attribute which had endeared her to the hearts of the great. Lord, but she could tell a tale or two.

She stirred the gruel until it was as smooth as silk, poured it into a silver dish, and placing the dish on a tray, together with a spoon, made her way from the kitchens and up to the

Princess's chamber. She found her patient wide awake and tossing restlessly, her cheeks flushed and damp.

Mrs. Griffiths put the gruel down hurriedly and ran to the bed. 'Your Highness? Is anything amiss?'

Charlotte gazed up at her, begging for the comfort of her knowledge and experience. 'Oh, Mrs. Griffiths, I have the most terrible pain in my belly, and I feel so hot.'

Mrs. Griffiths did not stay to comfort. She ran. Out of the bedroom and down the passage to alert Dr. Croft, which dogmatic gentleman, being completely satisfied that the Princess was in no danger, had retired for the night. Upon hearing the midwife's description of Charlotte's present condition, however, Dr. Croft rose with alacrity and dressed sloppily, not even bothering to put on a stock. Hopping along the passage with one boot on and the other in his hand, he progressed to Charlotte's bedroom. When she caught sight of the accoucheur Charlotte said at once, 'Oh,

Dr. Croft, such an awful pain! Did Mrs. Griffiths tell you?' She placed both hands on her stomach over the satin coverlet and looked up at him pleadingly, trustingly.

Dr. Croft, whose reputation was at stake with this most important patient, murmured placatingly, swallowed his pride and sent Mrs. Griffiths to wake Dr. Stockmar. Meanwhile he plied Charlotte with a large measure of brandy which she drank with shuddering distaste. When Stockmar came, a handsome young man, fair and Teutonic, wiping the sleep out of his eyes, Croft took him aside. 'I think she is bleeding internally,' he whispered.

'Dear God!' The German physician did not bother to hide his alarm. Croft pressed him. 'What do you advise?'

'I?' Stockmar looked surprised. He could not resist saying, 'I did not think my opinion was considered of any consequence in this matter.'

Dr. Croft ran his hands distractedly through his sparse grey hair. 'Devil take it, man. I have conquered *my* pride. Cannot you do likewise?'

Stockmar gave a quick nod. 'For her, yes, and for him too.'

'What is to be done then?'

The other considered the question carefully before pronouncing judgment. 'I think,' he said at last, 'that cold cloths applied to her abdomen might arrest the bleeding.'

The worthy doctor elevated his eyebrows. 'Do not you mean *hot* cloths?'

'No, indeed, Sir,' countered Stockmar firmly. 'Dr. Von Breughel of the University of Leyden has proved conclusively that the application of cold bags to the affected part will arrest internal haemorrhage more effectively than a hot poultice.'

But Dr. Croft was shaking his head. He was extremely doubtful. He preferred the tried and trusted methods. After all, the Princess might not be bleeding. She might simply be suffering from a severe attack of colic. He came to a decision, a compromise in deference to his fellow-physician, in whose opinion he had so very little faith. Indeed he would never have ventured to ask it had he not been so desperate. 'We will try my method first,' he declared, 'and if that is not effective we will try yours, Sir.' Saying which, the doctor beckoned to the worried Mrs. Griffiths and gave her the necessary orders, while Stockmar murmured to himself, 'If your methods fail, doctor, mine will not be needed.'

Stockmar approached the bed. Eagerly Charlotte seized his hand. 'Stocky, oh, Stocky,' her voice was querulous with fear.

'Your Highness?'

'Such an awful pain, Stocky.' How could she make them understand the extent of her discomfort? They did not seem to care that she was in the most dreadful agony! With his free hand Stockmar pushed back a damp tendril of hair clinging to her forehead. 'We will do all within our power to aid Your

Highness,' he soothed.

'I want Leopold.'

It was the cry of a child in the dark. He smiled down at her, for he must, if she was to survive, dispel the terror which had taken possession of her. 'Now, Highness,' he reproved, 'would it be kind of you to disturb the Prince for such a little thing? We shall have you more comfortable directly. Mrs. Griffiths is bringing hot cloths to place on your stomach. Come now, a little flatulence is no cause for waking a very tired man.'

She relaxed visibly, reassured by this simple diagnosis. She even managed to return his smile. 'Am I being a baby?'

'Well,' he conceded, 'we shall allow you a few hysterics, for you have undergone quite a long ordeal.'

'My poor little boy,' she commiserated. 'He is worse off than I.'

The hot cloths were brought and applied and yet another large measure of brandy was poured down Charlotte's throat. 'You are making me tipsy!' she complained and turning her head sideways upon the pillow, closed her eyes. Dr. Croft breathed a sigh of relief. She was responding to his treatment. He cast a triumphant glance at Stockmar who gave him a brief nod and walked towards the door.

'Stocky! Oh, Stocky!' He ran back to her side. She had raised herself on one elbow, her face contorted with pain. As he watched, speechless, powerless to aid her, she drew her knees up to her chin in a sudden, convulsive movement, rolled over on to her side and murmured the single word, 'Leopold.' It was quite a minute before Stockmar plucked up enough courage to feel for her non-existent pulse.

* * *

Upon hearing the terrible news from Claremont the Queen wrote to her eldest son:

'Bath, November 7 1817
My dearest Son,

How painful it is to me to take up my pen at this moment, when I had flattered myself to make use of it by giving you joy, which it had pleased the Almighty to change into grief and mourning for us all. I need not, I am sure, tell you that as I always share in your prosperity most sincerely, so do I most deeply feel your present loss and misery upon this melancholy event; and pray most anxiously to the Almighty that your health may not suffer from it. You must allow me to add to this that I rejoice in the comfort you must find of having had it in your power to make your child completely happy by granting her to marry the man she liked and wished to be united to, and who made her happy; as also upon the bestowing upon her a place at Esher she did enjoy with every possible gratitude and in which she spent to the very last almost complete felicity. These reflexions I do hope will alleviate your grief in some respects, as much as they give me real comfort upon your account.

Believe me, your most affectionate Mother,

Charlotte.'

Part Three

HAPPY AND GLORIOUS

BRUSSELS

December, 1817

It would have been cowardly of him not to tell her himself, and yet he found that it required a great deal of courage, even a measure of self-flagellation, before he could steel himself for the task. For the first time since the beginning of their long relationship, he waited for her with a feeling other than joyful anticipation, and mentally scourged himself again for his lack of guts.

She came running into the drawing-room, as beautiful as the day he had first met her, a small, dark, delicate-looking creature with astonishing violet eyes. Was she really only five years younger than he? He recalled a phrase he had once read in a book, something about the fire of eternal youth. The author must have been thinking of Madame de

St. Laurent when he wrote that, his Thérèse. She swept him a mocking curtsey, holding out her blue silk skirts, graceful as a bird. A smile touched the corners of her mouth. He kissed that mouth, and the old familiar scent of jasmine teased his nostrils, reminding him of nearly thirty years of tender fidelity, thirty years of married bliss, for he had married her, even though he had known that the simple ceremony in the Army chapel of the Gibraltar garrison would be invalidated by the Royal Marriage Act. He had done it to satisfy her almost puritanical views about the sanctity of their relationship.

Her eyes probed, marking the infinitessimal changes in his face since she had seen him last. 'You have not been to visit me for eight weeks, Edward. I did think you would be here for Christmas.' She noted the dark smudges under his eyes. 'You look tired, my dear.'

'Charlotte's death upset me,' he admitted.

She nodded understandingly. 'It was

unfortunate that the child was taken as well.'

'Yes.' And here was his opportunity to tell her. She had given him the perfect opening, but still his stupid tongue clove to the roof of his mouth and the words would not come. She tilted her head to one side, her eyes faintly puzzled and apprehensive, though she could not have said why she felt this insidious worm of fear beginning to crawl round her brain. So, in the end, it was she who had to find courage, courage to press him to reveal the nature of the unnameable something which was causing her heart to freeze. Even her valiant spirit could not summon up enough strength to ask outright if he had ceased to love her. She must take the roundabout route. She moved away from him, elegant in her high-waisted morning dress, and feeling that her legs might fail her, seated herself on a low chair before the fire, placing a face-screen between herself and the blazing logs, and thinking as she did so that she was behaving like the eternal whore who fears to damage her stock-in-trade. 'You were away for so long, Edward,' she complained. 'I thought you meant to come home directly after Charlotte's funeral.'

He stroked the velvet lapels of his tight-fitting frock-coat and walking over to her secretaire, picked up a miniature of himself painted by Beechey, the same who had immortalized Lord Nelson's mistress, Emma Hamilton, on so many canvasses. He studied it thoughtfully before answering, noting how the artist had minimized the protuberance of his eyes and the flabbiness of his wide, thick mouth. The miniature made him look distinguished and quite handsome, which he was not, never had been. Lawrence had done a better job on him in the full-length portrait which now hung in the Queen's Ballroom at Windsor. There, immortalized for all time, was the true Edward, Duke of Kent, a pot-bellied, rather pompous-looking soldier in full regimentals, with the blue Garter ribbon crossing his breast and George's portrait in miniature pinned to his shoulder, a portrait within a portrait, brother upon brother.

'Edward?' Her voice held a querulous, uncharacteristic note. He put down the miniature and started to fiddle with a vase containing several quill pens. 'George wanted me to stay and help to entertain the Saxe-Meiningen people,' he said at length. 'William is going to marry Adelaide of Saxe-Meiningen. He hopes to get a son by her. Now that Charlotte is dead there is no second generation heir-male.' Now! Tell her now! You are very close to the matter in hand, Edward. A single sentence will unburden you — and perhaps reduce her to a state of crushing misery.

She, for her part, could not bear to put off the moment any longer. 'And you, Edward?' she asked with an attempt at lightness. 'You must procreate for posterity too? Is that it? After William you are the next in line.'

He almost smiled, so great was his relief. 'I am to marry the Princess Louisa Maria Victoria of Saxe-Saalfeld-Coburg,' he blurted. 'She is the widow of Prince Emich of Leiningen and has one daughter.'

The colour fled from her cheeks. The shock was so great that she almost fainted. 'I see.' But she did not. She had thought only that he had stopped loving her, not that he had most foully betrayed her.

'I do not love her, of course,' Edward went on hurriedly, because he could not bear the look of pain in her eyes. 'I could never love anyone but you, Thérèse.'

'But you must protect the Hanoverian dynasty, must you not? It would never do for your mother's prodigious fecundity to go to waste.'

'Mama is very ill,' he said, as if that excused his underhanded behaviour in negotiating a marriage without her knowledge. 'The physicians say she will not live another year.'

She said nothing, offered no conventional expressions of sympathy for a woman who had always ignored her very existence. Instead she attacked him, pouring out the bitterness of years, repaying all the slights heaped upon her by the members of his family who did not approve of her, recalling the occasion when she had come to London with him, after his period of service in Quebec was over, and flinching even at this distance of time at the remembrance of the shabby little house in Hammersmith which she had been forced to occupy, so that the sight of her would not offend the Queen. Her tone was acid as she inquired, 'Have you any reason to suppose, my dear, that you will be able to father a child on your bride? In all our years of marriage, you have given me but two children.'

He bridled instantly, as would any man whose virility is being put at issue. 'I fathered six children before ever I met you, my dear.'

'You forgot to mention that I believe,

when you declared to me that you had never given yourself to another woman.'

'And would never have done so,' he blustered, 'if you had not goaded me into it.'

'I? Goaded you?' she flared. 'Did you not goad me? You come here, after an absence of eight weeks — during which time you sent me no word — and behave as though you have a hot coal in your breeches. I knew there was something wrong the moment I saw you. Your looks were mighty shifty for an innocent man.'

He was sweating now. He could feel the oily ooze of it trickling down the back of his neck. 'I came myself, did I not?' he returned hotly. 'I could have sent my equerry.'

She half rose from her chair, hands gripping the sides, her mouth ugly and distorted in anger, her violet eyes in a cat's glare. 'Why did not you then? I might have been able to offer my services to him. One discarded whore for sale at half price!' She began to weep, making him feel a mixture of anger, guilt and contrition. Damn George. Would it have been too much to ask that he sleep with Caroline until she gave him a boy? If he could only have persuaded her into bed once a week, he might have found her tolerable. He went and knelt before her, stiff and ponderous and faintly ridiculous. 'I never intended to desert you, Thérèse,' he pleaded. 'I shall always look to your welfare and visit you as often as I am able.'

She blew her nose. 'Do not forget to bring your wife!'

'Now, now,' he stroked her knee. 'Let us part friends, you and I.'

She looked down at the well-loved, so-familiar face, full now of entreaty, and her warm heart melted. He deserved nothing but pity for the circumstances which had forced him into what he plainly regarded as a distasteful marriage. She said: 'Do get up, Edward. You look rather silly, you know, and that humble posture is not good for your gout.' She added lightly, 'I must be grateful for all the years you have given me. *She* cannot take those away.'

The Duke of Kent unfolded his creaking joints. 'She can take nothing from you, my dear. For there is nothing to take. She will marry the shell of the man. You have the heart.'

CHELTENHAM

He had to see her one last time and yet he dared not let her see him, so he crept into the darkened theatre, unobtrusive in a brown redingcote and fawn breeches, a stout, middle-aged gentleman, whom nobody recognized. The usher showed him to his seat, which he quickly discovered to be damnably uncomfortable. But he stayed, doggedly ensconced, the heir to the throne of England, between two gentlemen of extremely doubtful origin, from whom emanated strange odours, which he could not immediately put a name to, though one, he could have sworn, was tar.

By the dim, flickering light of a flambeau, set on a pole in the centre aisle, he was able to discern the nature of the printed matter upon the programme. Under an engraving of a floating proscenium arch, upheld by naked cherubs and entwined with laurel leaves, he read, 'A performance of Shakespeare's 'Romeo and Juliet' by the Cheltenham Players, with Mr. Benjamin Archard as Romeo and Miss Susan Pillbury of Covent Garden Theatre, where she has lately been performing in the 'Beggar's Opera', as Juliet. Also appearing, will be Mrs. Dorothy Jordan as the Nurse to Juliet, this lady having been secured at great expense from the Theatre Royal, Drury Lane'.

What a lie! Dottie had not appeared at Drury Lane since before the fire. He felt a terrible pang of guilt. How was it possible that she, who had once been the toast of London, could be so reduced that she must play the role of a *servant* with a touring provincial theatre company? When he had left her in 1811 he had done the thing properly. He had met her at Cheltenham and discussed a settlement. She had been upset, of course, but even she had been forced to admit that they had nothing left to say to each other. They had ceased to be lovers after the birth of her tenth child. Sexually she was as drained as an empty barrel, played out, whereas he still had the urge and drive to pursue and make love to a pretty woman. She had known it, but she had wanted to hang on to him like any country housewife till death did them part. In the end she had agreed to four hundred pounds a year and a house in London, and one hundred pounds a year for the three younger children, who had yet to make their way in the world.

They had parted on reasonably friendly terms, and he had never thought to see her again. What in heaven's name had prompted him to come tonight to a flea-pit in Cheltenham? He could not say. He was on the threshold of a new life, about to embark upon legitimate matrimony with the wan-looking Adelaide, she of the spots and the pale yellow hair. She was amiable, he couldn't deny that, amiable and eager to please. The only trouble was, did she know how to please? He wondered gloomily what she would be like in bed and advised himself not to expect too much in that quarter, a virgin if ever he saw one. She was half his age though. She might learn. Dottie had known how to please him. When he broke with her he'd tried to get that saucy little piece, Catherine Tylney-Long, but she had already been offered elsewhere and at the time he made his application he had not been considered much of a catch. Young Charlotte had been very much alive, and kicking up the devil of a fuss about marrying Orange. Poor little devil. William's eyes filled with tears. What a thing to happen to a fine, strapping wench like her. One would have thought she could have had as many children as Mama without turning a hair. God moved in mysterious ways. Perhaps the Almighty had wanted him, William, to become King. He'd make a few changes if he outlived George. There'd be no more prodigal spending, no more creations of brick and mortar to inflame the people and make them hiss his carriage and throw things at him, as they did at George. He would be a model King. It did not occur to William that he was rather like the whore, who, having enjoyed life to the full, exploited to the limit every possible means of profitable self-indulgence, until she was too old to pursue her hectic course any further, had now, in her old age turned saint.

The man sitting on William's left was smoking a clay pipe. Wreaths of blue, evil-smelling smoke enveloped William's head. He coughed and waved it away with his rolled programme.

'Sorry, mate,' apologized his neighbour cheerfully. 'Keeps the bugs away don't'cha know.'

William shifted uneasily in his seat and immediately imagined he could feel an irritation in his crotch. He scratched it surreptitiously as a cheer went up from the audience, and the limelights having been ignited, the orchestra launched into the overture. William recoiled at the sound of an off-key violoncello, recalling with vivid clarity the night at the Brighton Pavilion when Rossini had played for them the overture from one of his operas, and George had performed with near-perfection upon that self-same instrument. His relief was heartfelt when the orchestra ground to a screeching, ragged halt and the curtain rose unevenly into the flies.

The scene was 'A public place in Verona', so poorly lit that he could see every brush-stroke on the painted backdrop, with its improbable colonnaded houses and even more improbable two-dimensional people clinging oddly to the façades. The performance, as he had expected, was excrutiatingly bad. He sat through two whole scenes before she appeared, making her entrance slowly in the wake of Lady Capulet. William felt rather sick. Was this stooping, raddled creature his beloved Dottie? God, it was only seven years since she had borne his last child. He stared at the heavily-rouged, sunken cheeks and the eyes, artificially bright with belladonna, watched the hesitant movements of her hands, the way she half limped across the stage as she made pretence to summon Juliet. It was clear that the audience felt cheated. They had all heard of the famous Dorothy Jordan, mistress to Prince William of Clarence, mother of ten FitzClarences. Could this be she? Or had the management conned them out of their two pence entrance fee with the substitution of an imposter? The hissing began, almost imperceptible at first, but rising quickly to a horrid crescendo. Boos and cat-calls followed, and then the first missile was thrown. Mrs. Dorothy Jordan, secured at great expense from the Theatre Royal, Drury Lane, precipitately left the stage, a tomato trapped incongruously in her white coif. William managed to get to the comparative security of his coach before he threw up.

HAMMERSMITH

1821

Over a year after her arrival in England, the Queen was still unable to shake off the feeling of nausea which had first taken possession of her during the abominable Channel crossing, a turbulent, erratic progress unusual for the month of June. She attributed her protracted malaise to the fact that she had remained in a continual state of nerves ever since she had received the intelligence that she was become Queen of England.

Lady Charlotte Campbell, who had been with the Queen in the old days at Blackheath, was helping her to dress in a gown of white satin with an overgown of silver lace, and to fix upon the garish yellow wig a slightly bent diamond tiara, which had not been cleaned since it had first nestled among the bronze curls of the old Duchess of Brunswick. Lady Charlotte secured the last silver hair-pin with a sigh of relief and stepped back slightly as Caroline gave a loud belch. She stepped back yet further to survey her handiwork and congratulated herself that she had done the very best she could with the meagre materials available.

At fifty-three Caroline of Brunswick had surrendered to the stoutness inherent in all the members of her family from the day of their birth, and the brilliant colouring she had once possessed was now vigorously counterfeited with paint, kohl and frequent applications of *poudré-papier*. It could not be denied that she bore an unfortunate resemblance to Mr. Punch's wife.

Her *toilette* completed, Caroline surveyed herself in the cheval-glass with wry amusement. She had always been able to laugh at herself. 'I present to you, ze Queen of England,' she declaimed, and added with her usual directness, 'I never thought zat old man at Vindsor vould die before George. Ze mad alvays live to a very great age, you know. It is God's vay of mocking His own creation. He holds up the mad like a mirror into vich man can look and see how foolish and vain he really is. Man does not like vat he sees, so he locks up ze mad, chains zem like vild beasts, and laughs at ze sight of zeir antics.' She turned to look directly at her friend. 'I haf it on good authority zat ze King is in very poor health. Is my informant to be believed?'

Lady Charlotte, who did not at all approve of what Caroline was about to do, answered with circumspection, 'He does suffer from gout, and of course, he is a little overweight.'

'A little overveight!' Caroline hooted with laughter. 'He is fat as a pig, and you know it, Lottie. I should not be surprised if he vere to get stuck in his Coronation chair. Vat a sight that vould be!' She threw up her hands in a gesture of incredulity. 'Did you ever hear of such a vain creature? They tell me he does not like ze expression of his face on ze new shilling piece lately issued. Brougham tells me he vill haf another one minted, bearing a face vith a more benign look.'

Lady Charlotte looked nervously about her as though she feared someone might overhear the shocking blasphemies issuing from the lips of the Queen of England. Caroline's rather eccentric life abroad had evidently not improved her demeanour. If possible, her manners were even more lax than before, her speech more coarse. Lady Charlotte had always liked Caroline in what she thought of as the 'Blackheath days', admiring her dauntless courage in the face of the terrible humiliations heaped upon her by her husband and the Queen. Now she didn't know. Caroline had changed a great deal, and there were those scandalous stories about her loose behaviour. Were any of them true, wondered Lady Charlotte? A year ago the King had instituted divorce proceedings against her. Witnesses, credible and suspect, had flocked in from Italy to testify in the House of Lords to the light conduct of the Queen, but in the end, nothing had been proved, and the judges had not granted the divorce. Caroline had come over from the Continent soon after she had heard of the death of George III, only to find herself the central figure in a drama which not even she could have imagined. With the aid of the ever-faithful Henry Brougham, she had defended herself ably in court, departing from thence with her honour intact. Now she was about to claim her rights as Queen and those rights included being crowned beside her husband.

When he had learned of his wife's intentions the King had stated unequivocally and publicly that he would not allow her to be crowned, and had given orders that her name was to be eradicated from the list of those members of the Royal family to be prayed for in church. If she attempted to enter Westminster Abbey on the day of his Coronation, the doors would be barred against her. As usual, the act of forbidding had the effect of hardening Caroline's determination to do the thing forbidden. Thus, she was preparing herself to go to the Abbey.

The Queen of England was still convulsed by her own witticism. 'Vat a sight that vould be!' she repeated. Then, seeing the expression of disapproval on Lady Charlotte's face, 'Ach, Lottie, vat a face! You frown upon my levity. Forgive me. If I vere not so scared I vould not say zese foolish sings.'

Lady Charlotte relented, charmed by Caroline's ability to analyze herself with such devastating accuracy. She did, however, venture to advise. 'Madam, I wish you would not go. They will bar the doors against you — and — insult you.'

'I know.' The Queen's face grew solemn. 'But I must go, you see. I must show him zat he still has a vife and zat his vife is ze Queen of England. If I hide myself, he can go smugly to his crowning and forget all about me. Zis way he vill remember. I vant him to remember — alvays, and as to being insulted, vell, I am used to zat.' She sighed regretfully. 'I could haf given him an heir, you know. I vas very fertile in my youth, but he hated me so. He vas drunk on our vedding night, and after he had consummated the marriage, he ran out of Carlton House and valked in ze gardens. Someone saw him vith his head in his hands and veeping most miserably. Vat a sing to remember! Zat your body vas so repulsive, it caused your husband to veep on his vedding night.' She shrugged off the wretched memory of that long-ago hurt, unaware that even her quaintly-pronounced English added a touch of the bizarre to an otherwise tragic situation. 'Now,' she continued, 'ze succession is still in some doubt. Only one little girl to follow his brother, Villiam.'

Lady Charlotte tried to strike a lighter note. 'She is an engaging moppet, but her mother keeps her very much apart from the Court. They say that Kensington Palace is protected like a fortress. The Duchess of Kent is so afraid that her little Vicky will become contaminated by contact with 'those awful wicked uncles' as she calls them.'

'Kent did not last long after he married her,' observed Caroline. 'Did his heart break at having to leave his actress?'

Lady Charlotte shook her head. 'I believe he had not been well for some time before he married. It might have been the final straw.'

'So now zere are only eleven.'

'Eleven, Madam?'

Caroline tugged at the neck of her bodice which, cutting into her ample flesh, marked her breasts with a red line. 'Eleven of Charlotte Sophia's brood,' she explained. 'She vas fortunate. Her maternal instincts vere indulged to the full, and she did not live to see any of her children die a painful death ven she vas not by to comfort zem.'

'Oh, Ma'am!' Lady Charlotte stretched out a sympathetic hand. 'It must have been a terrible blow for you.'

'I blame myself for leaving her.'

'You could not have changed the course of events, Ma'am, and . . . '

'And he vould not let me be a mother to her anyvay. That is vat you vere about to say, is it not?' Seeing the distress on her friend's face, Caroline made a small despairing gesture with her hands. 'Ach, Gott, let it go. It is all done now. Come, Lottie, let us storm ze portals of ze enemy.'

★　★　★

The journey to the Abbey was a nightmare for Lady Charlotte. The decorated streets, with their floral arches and elaborate, painted columns were lined with people, who mobbed the coach as they recognized its flamboyant occupant. Caroline, not a whit put out, nodded and smiled as people pressed round the sides of the vehicle and peered into the windows. Lady Charlotte shuddered as each common, ugly face, framed by the window, disappeared, only to be immediately replaced by yet another, commoner, uglier face, rubicund, dirty and gap-toothed. But these were friendly faces. How much more terrible would it be if they were not. What must it have been like for Queen Marie Antoinette, riding in an open cart through Paris, her hands tied behind her back, to that dreadful, humiliating death? What a craven creature you are, Charlotte, she admonished herself.

The coachman drew up at the great west door of Westminster Abbey, about which the crowd milled, thicker than ever. Caroline put her hand on Lady Charlotte's knee. 'Stay here, Charlotte. This vill not take long, and zere is no need for you to suffer a buffeting.'

Lady Charlotte nodded gratefully, thoroughly ashamed of her own temerity. The coachman was holding open the door. Caroline stepped down and the crowd, silent and respectful, parted like the Red Sea before Moses. Slowly she walked towards the door, which was shut, and guarded by two sentries. Politely they asked to see her pass. She said, 'I haf no pass. I am ze Queen of England. I am come to be crowned.'

'I am sorry, Ma'am, but you may not go in,' replied he on the right of her. 'The King's instructions were explicit.'

'I haf no doubt they vere.' She smiled at them uncertainly. The smile wobbled and died, and then Caroline of Brunswick, Queen of England, sat down on the cobbles of the forecourt and wept most bitterly, watched by the sympathetic crowd.

Back in the coach, she wiped her eyes, removed her tiara and said, 'Zis vill kill me. He has done for me at last. It is ze final degradation.'

WINDSOR

1828

The King limped to his phaeton, assisted by Captain Wilkie McMahon, his principal equerry, and followed by Lady Conyngham, his mistress. Surrounding Thatched Cottage, a high 'wall' of privet protected Majesty from the vulgar public gaze, so that his unloving subjects should not see the pathetic picture he made as, crippled with gout, burdened with fat, and trembling from the effects of too much brandy, he prepared for his daily outing, taking with him a huge silver chamberpot engraved with his arms, to accommodate the frequent and erratic demands of his waterworks. To add to the King's misery, every time he did pass water, in slow, irritating dribbles, the pain half killed him.

The equerry, sweat beading his brow, finally succeeded in wedging the King into the phaeton, leaving barely enough room for Lady Conyngham to dispose her substantial bulk, and all were ready to depart for the afternoon ride. The King, wheezing with the effort of climbing into the vehicle, accepted the long whip from Captain McMahon, touched up the two bays, and they were off, the lady with a proprietary hand upon Majesty's left knee.

Lady Conyngham enjoyed her position as *maitresse en titre*, especially since it did not necessitate sharing the King's bed. Her duties were confined to the giving of comfort on the King's 'bad days', when his gout troubled him more than usual, and his weak bladder prompted miserably long sessions on his commode. She queened it, a platonic Pompadour, at Windsor and at Brighton, but more often at Windsor now, where the King could hide from the hatred and ridicule of his subjects. With Lady Jersey and Lady Hertford relegated to the dim and distant past, and Maria Fitzherbert in failing health at Brighton, Lady Conyngham reigned supreme.

Meanwhile, the King, his bronchial tubes slowly relaxing, was in sombre mood. Two days ago he had received word from Würtemberg that his eldest sister had died after an attack of influenza. This, coming so soon after the death of his favourite brother, Frederick, Duke of York, had made him feel depressed and out of sorts. The family was dwindling. Charlotte Sophia's progeny now numbered a mere nine, and he was feeling so devilish pukey these days that he greatly feared it would very soon number but eight.

These gloomy thoughts, mulled over to the even trotting rhythm of the horses, so obsessed the King that he drove much farther than he had intended, and was surprised to find himself fetching up at the Fishing Temple at Virginia Water. He experienced a moment's panic. What if he should run into a party of schoolboys from Eton, who, not content with making mock of him, would run behind the phaeton all the way back to Thatched Cottage and damn near give him a seizure with their impudence? Anger, that ancient enemy of fear, came to his rescue. Damned if he'd turn tail. Let anyone bait him who dared. He'd see 'em off with his whip.

At sight of the King's gay little equipage, a few old men fishing desultorily, rose from their perches by the side of the lake and stood up to bow to him. He accorded them a gracious inclination of his head, quite pleased at this mark of civility. There were so few of them, of course. It was only when people were assembled in large numbers that they dared openly to voice their opinions of him and throw mud at his carriage. Cowards at heart they were, picking on him when he was forced to drive through their midst. The King felt a keen sense of injury when he thought of the treatment he received at the hands of his subjects. It had all stemmed from his relations with Caroline, now dead, thank God. Right from the first they had taken her part, not knowing how distasteful he found it to consort with a creature so indecorous and loud-mouthed as she, not to mention her insanitary habits! He always felt too that the people blamed him for his daughter's death, as though he could, in some way, have prevented what had happened to her. The mob was a curious, fickle animal. Given the right circumstances, it could just as soon reverse its opinion of him and take him to its heart. Perhaps it needed another Waterloo to make him popular.

The King knew himself to be a man of wide and varied talents. Was he not a very competent musician? Was he not Europe's most accomplished connoisseur of art? Had he not been among the very few who had appreciated the bringing to England of Lord Elgin's marbles? Had he not paid for the Apollo Belvedere, and other statues filched by

Napoleon, to be transported back to Rome and restored to their rightful places, instead of accepting them as a gift from the Pope, as he might have done? One could expect the common herd to appreciate that indeed! All they thought about were his past indiscretions, his wild youth, and the enormous sums of money he had spent in building and altering fine houses, monuments to immortalize him, since he had no child to give him immortality.

Lady Conyngham was tapping his knee, trying to engage his attention. 'Your Majesty, I think that is the carriage of the Duchess of Kent.'

He squinted in the direction of his companion's discreetly pointing finger and saw, plainly displayed upon the side of an elegant landau, his brother's coat-of-arms impaled with those of Saxe-Saalfeld-Coburg. He felt even more gloomy. An encounter with the formidable Victoria, Duchess of Kent, was not his idea of an entertaining interlude in the dull daily round. He'd quite forgotten that she was staying with Gussie at Frogmore, else he'd never have ventured out. Speak to her he must, however, for she had spotted him too and, with her usual grim adherence to the rules of protocol, was waiting for him to approach her. With a grunt of disgust, he set the horses in motion and trotted round to the other side of the pond, noting as he did so that the Duchess had with her her nine-year-old daughter, the Princess Victoria. The King did not like children. He could never manage to come down to their level, and they always made him nervous by staring at him. The distinct impression was given that they would very much like to stick out their tongues in derision.

From the distant bandstand he could hear the musicians striking up a march. After this ordeal was over he'd go and sit by the bandstand for a while and listen to the music. He reined in the horses, pulling up expertly alongside the Duchess's landau. Confound him if she didn't look a fright. All that black hair arranged in floppy ringlets, and her cheeks rouged, and God knows, someone should stop her from wearing green satin!

As usual the child was staring at him, a plain-faced little thing, but with rather arresting blue eyes and a small mouth curving into a smile, taking him by surprise. The smile gave the little face an unnatural maturity. 'Good afternoon, Uncle,' piped this diminutive creature. He smiled back at her. 'Good afternoon, Vicky. Taking the air, I see.' His eyes went to the Duchess. Why did she always wear that air of offended indignation? Was it only he who invoked it, or did she wear it permanently? Anyone would have thought he had just made an improper suggestion. No wonder Edward had given up the ghost after two years of marriage to her. Died of boredom probably.

Something of what he was thinking must have showed on the King's face because her dark eyes took on a look of hard reproach as she made her conventional greeting, 'Good afternoon, Your Majesty.' He responded in kind and inquired after her health, which he learned was fair, in spite of a bad cold which had kept her confined to her bed for three days, and from which she was just now recovering. This subject being disposed of the King was at a loss. How to bring the uncomfortable interview to a conclusion and be on his way? Vicky, sensing no constraint whatsoever between Mama and Uncle King, volunteered the information that she would like to listen to the band, whereupon the Duchess intervened to say sharply, 'It is time to go home to tea, Victoria. You may listen to the band another day.'

The unspoken, but patently obvious proviso, was that she might do so when Uncle King was safely shut up in Thatched Cottage. Victoria looked disappointed but submitted with a meek, 'Yes, Mama.' The little contretemps injected a spark of devilment into the King, always latent, very long unused. Ever on his mettle where his sister-in-law was concerned, he argued loudly, 'Of course she may listen to the band, Ma'am. I was about to do so myself.'

The red lips of the Duchess tightened like a trap. 'You will forgive me, Sir, but I think I know what is best where my own daughter is concerned. We shall go home to tea.'

The King squared his shoulders. He was beginning to enjoy himself. 'You may not disobey a royal command, Ma'am,' he pointed out with sweet reasonableness, 'and as to *your* daughter, may I remind you that she is also *my* niece, and that having been born to such a high position she may not be regarded as exclusively your property. You, Ma'am, are not a cottager's wife and she is not a common child. One day she will wear my crown.'

Vicky looked startled and the Duchess outraged. The King met his niece's astonished gaze and narrowed his eyes. Angrily he addressed his sister-in-law. 'I see you have been derelict in your duty, Ma'am. It is time she knew.'

The Duchess tried hard to hold on to the rags of her self-control. 'I do not think it prudent at this time,' she replied stiffly. 'It would not do for the child to get above herself.'

'Or above you, eh, Ma'am?' he shot back, and had the satisfaction of seeing his shaft go home as the black eyes widened into a fixed glare. He had not enjoyed himself so much since he'd cut Brummell in Calais. Regally he instructed her, 'Tell her as soon as you get back to Kensington, Ma'am. If you do not, I shall. I shall send McMahon, my equerry, to confirm that you have done so. Now then, pop Vicky into my carriage. We are going to listen to the band and she may sit on Lady Conyngham's lap. Pop her in.'

The defeated Duchess, who had not so far acknowledged the presence of Lady Conyngham, visibly recoiled at the notion of her precious child coming into physical contact with one of her brother-in-law's kept women, but she saw by the glint in the King's eye that his blood was up and that he did not intend to be thwarted. When the Great Mahomet was in this mood there was no gainsaying him. Well, today had taught her a lesson. Never again would she ride out as far as the Fishing Temple. Reluctantly she prompted the willing Vicky to rise, and helped her cross over into the King's phaeton, wincing as the little girl bounced on to Lady Conyngham's knee and smiled up into that lady's face. The Duchess positively blenched as Lady Conyngham bent down to kiss her dear, pure little Vicky.

'We're off, then!' exclaimed the King boyishly, and with a brief, triumphant salute to the Duchess he whipped up the bays. 'What shall we ask the band to play, m'dear?' he inquired genially of his niece.

She dimpled prettily, burst out

laughing in a way which gave him a sharp stab of agony, so much did it remind him of Charlotte, and said, 'Why Sir, 'God Save the King', if you please.'

THE PAVILION, BRIGHTON

1833

Mrs. Fitzherbert felt very tired. She knew the King meant to be kind, but she did wish he would refrain from mentioning subjects which were painful to her and which brought back so many half-buried memories. George was dead now and very soon she would join him, though not, as she had hoped, at Windsor. That would certainly overstep the bounds of propriety, even though Caroline had been interred in her native Brunswick. She looked at the short, stout man sitting opposite to her, legs splayed, hands gesticulating, face as rubicund as a cherry. George's brother, now occupying George's place, and that place to be occupied later by the single legitimate girl produced by Charlotte

Sophia's nine sons. One might almost regard it as a judgement on their profligacy. Maria believed in judgements.

' . . . and I say that the marriage certificate should be published, Ma'am, to give the lie to those who say you were never actually united to my brother.' These words reached Mrs. Fitzherbert through the swirling fog of memories clouding her brain, which had been brought into life by the King's reminiscences.

'Oh, no, no, sir.' Her grey eyes showed alarm. 'I have no mind to stir up a turmoil now that he is gone. He would not have liked that at all.'

Queen Adelaide, tall, slender and colourless, put in gently, 'He died with your miniature about his neck, Ma'am, and your letter beneath his pillow. He wanted you to have this.' So saying, the Queen unclasped her reticule and delving within took out a signet ring set with a tiny painted miniaure of an eye, which she held out towards Maria.

Maria recognized it at once. She had its fellow on the third finger of her left hand, above her wedding band. That vulgar little fellow Richard Cosway had painted the twin miniatures, George's eye on her ring, her eye on George's ring. Her hand shook as she took the ring from Adelaide and placed it beside the other. The two eyes looked incongruous, one above the other, on her finger. She wanted to weep. Then she wanted to laugh. Maria compromised and smiled at the gentle Queen, who recognized another woman's need for such soothing placebos. 'He did not reply to my letter,' she said, trying to control her quivering mouth. 'I wish I could have received one last word from him.'

'The rogue!' blustered William. 'He used you ill, Ma'am, and now you would defend him. Your forbearance is remarkable.'

Again it was the Queen who brought Maria comfort. 'He was too ill to write, Ma'am,' Adelaide explained. 'He could not even lift a pen, so weak was he at the last, but he cherished your letter, I know. He had it by him all the time.'

Maria smiled her grateful thanks, secretly pitying the Queen in her role as placator to the fiery little man beside her. She must have the patience of Griselda. In an attempt to turn the subject of their conversation away from herself and her dead lover, whom the King seemed determined to resurrect, in order that he might revile him, whereas she thought only of the happiness George had brought her, she inquired after the members of the Royal family and learned that all were at present in pretty fair health, that Augustus had married the Lady Cecilia Underwood, that Cumberland was in Hanover and that the Princess Mary was 'cat-and-dogging' it with her husband, the Duke of Gloucester. His sister's somewhat frantic domestic situation seemed to afford the King a great deal of enjoyment in contemplation, though Mary was, without a doubt, suffering at the hands of the Duke. Maria deplored this lack of feeling on his part, but offered no comment as he recounted horrid tales of marital strife. Her heart sank as William said bluntly, 'You and George never had any children. Dam'me if I don't think that deuced odd, Ma'am, you being so much in each other's company in the old days.'

Maria looked down at her hands, old and wrinkled in her satin lap. 'I miscarried twice,' she admitted. 'Perhaps God in His wisdom was merciful.'

William was visibly shaken. George had never breathed a word. 'Yes, yes,' he agreed hurriedly and thought about Mrs. Fitzherbert's marriage certificate which he was so eager to publish. If she'd had a couple of boys and a good lawyer, a slippery fellow like Brougham, for instance, quite a nasty situation could have arisen. It was he now who tried to strike a different note. 'D'ye remember, Ma'am when you and George were first married and living at

Park Street, how we used to come in, roaring drunk, to find you hiding under the sofa?'

Maria bit her lip. She remembered, only too well, the way George would run to snatch a sword from his closet and tease her with it, yelling, 'I'll flush you out, my beauty, you'll not escape me!' in the prescribed manner of a stage villain. Yes, she remembered. In her mind's eye the beloved image was sharply, agonizingly perceptible, the blue eyes shining with mischief, the cheeks more than usually flushed, the fair hair in elegant disarray.

'Yes,' she admitted in a small voice, 'I recall those days very well, Sir, better perhaps than I remember what I did last week, which I daresay was quite unremarkable.'

'Well, dam'me, Ma'am,' William slapped his knee. 'Why d'ye not come to Court and mingle with the Queen's ladies? Take ye out of y'self. Ye must be lonely living in that house over yonder.'

Did he realize just how lonely, she

wondered? She declined his offer, making excuse that she was too old to become part of the social round, and William, a little put out by her steadfast negation of his pressing suggestions, rose to indicate that the interview was at an end, and that she might retire to the seclusion of her own house.

She went, managing a dignified curtsey, and reflecting wryly upon the turn of fortune's wheel. At one time the Pavilion had been her domain. She had had her own apartments, and when George came down, his guests had accommodated themselves to her wishes, not she to theirs.

William watched her go and shrugged. 'Damned woman's stubborn,' he remarked to his wife. Adelaide the peace-maker leapt to Maria's defence. 'She is very old, William.'

'Stubborn as a mule,' he insisted and lit his pipe.

PORTLAND PLACE

1833

The Princesses Augusta and Sophia arrived early for Mary's 'At Home', thinking it would be pleasant to discuss family topics until the other ladies arrived, but when their carriages pulled up and they entered the house, they found their sister close to hysterics and pounding on the door of her drawing-room, with a frightened footman at her elbow attempting to restrain her. When Mary caught sight of her sisters coming towards her across the marble floor she turned, tears streaming down her cheeks, and flung herself bodily at Sophia, carefully choosing she from whom the most sympathy could be expected.

Sophia embraced her sister, patting her back and murmuring words of comfort for she knew not what. 'There, there, dear, what is it?'

Mary swallowed down a rising sob and wailed, 'He has locked me out of my drawing-room! He — he says it is untidy and not fit to be seen by my guests. I shall be forced to receive on the top floor. Oh, what will everyone *think*!'

'If you tell them the truth they will think you have a pig for a husband,' stated Augusta, who prided herself on being a 'Sally Blunt', and privately thought her sister a weak fish to put up with Silly Billy's caperings. 'I should not say a word if I were you,' she advised. 'London society knows a great deal more about our private affairs than is good for it, we having such unreliable servants these days.' She glared unfairly at the young footman, who smiled at her nervously. Pointing to the drawing-room doors, Augusta asked, 'Is he in there?'

Mary nodded wordlessly, still clinging to Sophia, whereupon her elder sister marched up to the door and bending down, bellowed through the keyhole, 'Come on out, Cheese, or shall I send for the King? He is at the palace, you know, and can be here in half an hour. He will have you out in very short order!'

Gloucester, who detested being called by his vulgar nickname of 'Cheese', rather more than he detested being dubbed 'Silly Billy', called back, 'If that's you, Gussie, you can go to hell, and take your blubbering sister with you. She's no good to me, the old crow.'

'He's drunk,' opined Augusta flatly, as if that explained everything. She glanced at her watch, hanging by a silk strap from her bodice. There was just ten minutes to go before the guests began arriving. 'Give him the victory,' she counselled the tearful Mary. 'He is not worth getting in a state about, and if anyone asks why you are entertaining upstairs, tell 'em to mind their own business.'

Reluctantly Mary agreed and dully instructed the footman to show the ladies to the Upper Saloon. As she and her sisters mounted the stairs, Augusta commented caustically, 'His grandmother was a rag-and-bone woman. What can one expect? You were a fool to marry him, Mary.'

Mary dabbed at her face with her handkerchief and patted her false yellow curls. 'I *know*, Gussie,' she returned with some spirit. 'I should have lived in sin, like you, till I tired of him.'

Augusta leapt to her own defence. 'Brigadier-General Brent Spencer and I were in love when we began our liaison,' she said loftily. 'You were never in love with 'Cheese', so do not make pretence that you were.'

Mary started to cry again. 'Do not call him that dreadful name, Gussie, if you please. Do not, I beg you.'

'Oh, for heaven's sake!' Sophia's patience with her sisters ran out. 'We are all too old to wrangle.'

'Yes, so we are,' agreed Mary tiredly. 'We were never young it seems to me.'

The Duchess of Gloucester began

receiving precisely at three o'clock. Lady Mountjoy, always the first-comer, stick-thin, the bodice of her gown padded with horse-hair, curtseyed to Mary and remarked upon the strange noises issuing from the drawing-room below.

'What sort of noises, Ma'am?' Mary asked faintly.

'Well,' Lady Mountjoy's pointed nose twitched, scenting the beginnings of a most delightful little tale to be recounted later to her friends. She waved her hands in the air, 'Thumping and banging, and . . . er,' she hesitated, puzzled and titillated by the Princess's agitated manner, 'I . . . er, I think I heard the sound of breaking glass and someone . . . er, swearing *most dreadfully!*'

'Oh, the painters,' put in the resourceful Augusta, with a breeziness which disappointingly dispelled any suggestion of a scandal. 'I advised you to take all the breakables out of the drawing-room, Mary.'

'Yes, Augusta, so you did,' replied Mary meekly.

'So that's it? Tipsy painters!' laughed Lady Doddington, a round little dowager wearing spectacles. 'Your Highness must engage my decorator, Mr. Coxall. He is the most careful of men.'

The talk ebbed and flowed, and Mary relaxed. The Reform Bill was discussed, Lady Mountjoy giving her unsolicited opinion that — Lord knew what would happen now that every Tom, Dick and Harry was represented in Parliament.

Augusta took her up on this at once, noting that it was just like the Mountjoy to wear feathers in the afternoon. 'My brother, the King,' she declared firmly, 'worked long and hard to encourage the reform of the rotten boroughs. The Reform Bill is an excellent measure.'

'I hear that Lord Melbourne is thinking of retiring,' interposed the Duchess of Newcastle, seeing the light of battle in Augusta's eye and tactfully trying to avoid a clash. Augusta, easily diverted by any tittle of gossip concerning someone not in her immediate family circle, trilled with laughter. 'You are more than usually gullible if you believe that, Your Grace. The truth is that the King is tired of his political acrobatics and is about to throw him out of office.'

'Really?' The Duchess flicked open her fan. 'And I thought him the most agreeable man alive!'

'Looks are very often deceptive,' observed Augusta darkly. Out of the corner of her eye she saw Mary beckoning to her from the door and excusing herself, went to join her sister. Mary grabbed her arm. 'Lord, Gussie. William's valet says that William has come out of the drawing-room and has collapsed in the hall.'

'Drunken sot!' snorted Augusta.

'No, no,' Mary's hand fluttered nervously. 'You mistake my meaning. John says he thinks that William has had some sort of seizure. Come down with me, Gussie, pray do.'

Augusta cast a quick glance over her shoulder, conscious of the impropriety of leaving guests to their own devices. Sophia was there to hold the fort, however, and the matter did seem urgent. She therefore accompanied Mary downstairs to the hall. One look at Gloucester convinced Augusta that he was suffering from something other than an excess of alcohol. He was lying on his back with his mouth hanging open, breathing in quick little gasps. The skin of his face was bedewed with perspiration and of a purplish-red hue. His small eyes glittered through half-lowered lids. Augusta viewed him with distaste. 'You had better send for the physician,' she told her sister. 'I think he has had an attack of apoplexy.' She added with her usual directness, 'Perhaps your prison bars are about to break, my dear.'

June 28, 1838

On the day of Queen Victoria's Coronation, Mr. Charles Greville, that indefatigable recorder of events both momentous and unremarkable, returned home, physically exhausted, and wrote in his diary:

'The Coronation (which, thank God, is over) went off very well. The day was fine without heat or rain — an innumerable multitude which thronged the streets orderly and satisfying. The appearance of the Abbey was beautiful, particularly the benches of the peeresses which were blazing with diamonds. The Queen looked very diminutive and the effect of the procession itself was spoiled by being too crowded; there was not enough room between the Queen and the Lords and others going before her. The Bishop of London preached a very good sermon. The different parts in the ceremonial were very imperfect and it was obviously unrehearsed. Lord John Thynne, who officiated for the Dean of

Westminster, told me that nobody knew what was to be done except the Archbishop and himself (who had rehearsed), Lord Willoughby (who is experienced in these matters) and the Duke of Wellington and consequently there was continual difficulty and the Queen never knew what she was to do next.

'They made her leave her chair and enter into St. Edward's Chapel before the prayers were concluded, much to the discomfort of the Archbishop. She said to Sir John Thynne, 'Pray tell me what I am to do, for they do not know' — and at the end, when the orb was put into her hand, she said to him, 'What am I to do with it?' 'You are to hold on to it, Ma'am,' he instructed. The Queen said, 'Am I?' and she added, 'It is very heavy.' The ruby ring was made for her little finger instead of the fourth one which the rubric prescribes that it should be for. When the Archbishop was to put it on she extended the former, but he said it must be the latter. She said it was too small and she could not get it on. He said it must go on the fourth finger and forced it on so that when she came to take it off after the ceremony she was obliged to bathe her finger in water to get it off.

'I went into the park afterwards where a fair was going on and a vast multitude was assembled, mainly of the lower orders. The great merit of the Coronation is that so much has been done for the people — to amuse and interest them seems to have been the principal object.'

★   ★   ★

On October 8 1839 the Queen wrote a single sentence in her diary: 'Albert is beautiful.'

1840

'So Vicky is to marry Albert of Saxe-Coburg,' said Augusta. 'I shall not be at the ceremony, my dears. I feel too unwell for such exertions.'

'He is very handsome,' put in Sophia, the romantic.

'He is a little like Leopold,' said Mary and added, 'I wonder if Vicky will have as many children as poor, dear Mama?'

'We wondered that about Charlotte,' Augusta reminded her. 'It does not do to count one's chickens.'

Sophia gave vent to a long, reminiscent sigh. 'She is very much in love.'

'She is in love with the idea of being in love,' Augusta corrected her sister firmly. 'Still, I suppose a German prince is a distinct improvement on that fop Melbourne.'

'Oh, Gussie,' Sophia remonstrated. 'Vicky was never in love with Lord Melbourne.'

'Then she gave a very good imitation of it,' came the snappish retort. 'Bawling when he fell out of office, dancing with joy when he got back in. Did you ever hear of such capers?'

'A husband will set all to rights,'

prophesied Sophia complacently.

'Would it not be strange,' mused Mary, 'if Vicky should have as many children as Mama. Does not the thought of history repeating itself in such a way amuse you, my dears?'

Augusta directed a withering look at Mary, closed her eyes and lay back in her chair.

BUCKINGHAM PALACE

1857

They poured a hot toddy down her throat, put hot bottles at her feet — new-fangled stone things filled with boiling water — and left her to sleep, the Queen showing her usual sweet concern over the indisposition of a relative. But Mary, Duchess of Gloucester, could not sleep, and after an hour of restless tossing from side to side, she gave up the struggle, abandoned her legion of sheep, and heaving herself out of bed, donned a night-wrapper. As she tied the neck ribbons with her clumsy, gnarled fingers she shivered slightly, for the room was cold. The Queen would never permit the lighting of fires in the bedrooms. She regarded this habit as most unhealthful and self-indulgent and moreover, a highly dangerous procedure, since when one was asleep, with the bed-curtains drawn, one could not possibly see whether or not a spark might fly out of the fire and ignite the carpet.

Mary moved over to a small secretaire which contained all her private papers. She was quite lucid now after her temporary aberration, though imbued with an odd sense of unreality, as though poised delicately between the then and the now, and not knowing whether to step into the past or to remain firmly established in the present. From the top of the secretaire she picked up a porcelain vase, shaped like a fish standing on its tail, and extracted from its convuluted interior a silver key. With this she opened the bottom right-hand drawer of the secretaire.

Some instinct, premonition, nostalgic longing, call it what you will, was prompting her to look at her diaries. There were eight of them, covering a period of forty years, five years of family history painstakingly recorded in each leather-bound book. She took them out, one by one, and opening the flap of the secretaire, laid them before her, enjoying the feel of the smooth leather under her fingers, tracing with a forefinger her coat-of-arms embossed in gold on the front of the one dated 1817 – 1822.

She opened it, riffling through the pages until she came to the entry for the seventh of November, 1817. It read: 'Lord Liverpool came to my house at six o'clock this evening and brought me the terrible news of Charlotte's death, which took place at Claremont on the sixth day of November at 2.30 a.m., two days after the demise of her child. At first, I could scarce comprehend what he was saying to me and when at length I perceived that this dreadful circumstance had indeed come to pass, I fell to weeping. Lord Liverpool kindly inquired if my husband were at home. I said he was not, for I would not have William torn away from his drunken slumbers. He would have proved of little comfort to me. Lord Liverpool told me that the embalmers had been sent down to Claremont, but that Leopold had refused to let them perform their work, saying that he would not have his darling mutilated in death. It was Dr. Stockmar who persuaded Leopold of the necessity of this doleful ritual, pointing out that he might not interfere with the traditions of the English Royal Family. Very right and proper, though I must say that I sympathize with the bereaved husband most heartily. The funeral is to take place at Windsor on the eighteenth day of this month.'

She stared at her own handwriting, faded now to a brownish-yellow. The remembrance of that unlooked-for tragedy, which had taken place forty years ago, still had the power to move her. She wiped her eyes with her sleeve and turning the pages of the diary came to an entry in January of the year 1818. A smile flitted across her lips. A bare statement of fact recorded the marriage of her brother,

William, Duke of Clarence, to Adelaide of Saxe-Meiningen and that of her brother Edward to Louisa Maria Victoria of Saxe-Saalfeld-Coburg. Hurried, arranged marriages those, in a desperate bid to get an heir for the House of Hanover. Three children, all girls, had been born of the two unions. Only one had survived. In 1818, too, her sister Elizabeth had married the Landgrave of Hesse-Homburg. Ah, yes, here it was — May 16 1818: 'Elizabeth was married today to her 'Bluff' as she calls him. What a spectacle she made of herself in silver tissue and lace, like a young bride, and she all of forty-eight years. I fear everyone was laughing at her, and to make matters worse, when the ceremony was done, that fat buffoon of a man bent down to pick up Mama's fan, which she had inadvertently let fall, and in the process split his breeches. I swear you could have heard the crack at Land's End.' Poor Lizzie, her 'Bluff' had died eleven years to the day after her marriage, and her ecstatic letters home had proved that they had been happy years for her. No more than her due.

She turned the pages and found the entry recording her mother's death: November 17 — 'Mama died very peacefully in her sleep at three o'clock this morning. Though I wept, I could not regret that she, who had been suffering so much pain, should at last be released and taken to the bosom of Christ.' Mama had never really recovered from the shock of Charlotte's death.

The remainder of the diary seemed to be a record of births and deaths. In 1819 Vicky had been born, and eight months later there were entries concerning the death of Vicky's father, Edward Duke of Kent, and of the King. Papa. She had not been able to shed a single tear for him. To her and to her sisters, he had died long, long before the breath left his body. Only the shell of the man had remained to haunt Windsor, a shell to be hastily thrust away in some remote chamber, if George should chance to entertain foreign visitors there.

Mary put aside the diary, stroking it as though it were an old friend, and picked up the one dated 1822 – 1826. Nothing much here. George was King and had made several state visits — to Ireland, to Scotland and to Hanover. He had also travelled to Belgium, where Wellington had accompanied him on a guided tour of the field of Waterloo, and had shown him the very tree under which Lord Uxbridge's leg was buried. In 1824 she had noted the sinking of the first pile of London Bridge.

In the next diary the death of the Duke of York was entered in January and in February there was an interesting item about Sir Walter Scott, who had at last 'confessed' to the authorship of the Waverley Novels. Conceited ass. Mary pulled a face. Everyone knew he was the author anyway. Why make such a song and dance about it? How that wretched man had taken and taken from George, and how he had ridiculed him behind his back, calling him 'Old Prinny' and other, less kind epithets.

The fourth diary reminded her of Royal's death and she was surprised to read her own laconic entry: 'Charlotte Augusta died at the palace of Würtemberg at eleven o'clock on Friday.' Had she felt nothing at the time? Perhaps not. Royal had not been a part of her life for thirty-one years before her death. To do her justice, Royal had been an assiduous letter-writer, but she did tend to harp on trivialities and quite often one must set aside her letters, after reading the first two pages, from veritable boredom.

The great event of the year 1830 had been the death of her brother George and the accession of William. She had made a note of William's odd behaviour at George's funeral: 'William walked behind the gun-carriage, actually laughing with the Duke of Wellington, who seemed mighty astonished by such behaviour, but did not like to offend by keeping a correctly solemn countenance. It appears that William is so pleased to be King that even George's death has not the power to affect his spirits. Augusta, the 'Sally Blunt' of our family, rebuked him afterwards, and he had the grace to look ashamed, though not for long. He was very soon talking about the arrangements for his Coronation and declaring his intention of pulling down the cottage at Windsor where George lived with Lady Conyngham during the latter part of his life. This is a house detested by the people because, for some reason that I do not understand, they have come to regard it as a symbol of George's prodigality. I should have thought the Pavilion fitted that role better. George was not loved by his people. Will William be loved I wonder? He is determined to go down to Brighton very soon and 'reinstate' Mrs. Fitzherbert. He thinks she has been treated shamefully. I do not. She knew when she married George that nothing but bad could come of such a union. From what I know of the lady she will not take kindly to William's patronizing. It worries me to think that there is no male heir. I suppose we must get used to the idea of looking upon little Vicky as our future Queen. Such a heavy weight of responsibility to be put upon such a *very small person*.'

For her, 1831 had seen nothing more remarkable than the marriage of her brother Augustus, Duke of Sussex, to the Lady Cecilia Underwood. Mama would have considered that another unsuitable marriage, but by that time it had mattered little. Vicky had been a strong little girl of ten, and there was no reason to suppose that she would not succeed William, marry and bear children for the succession.

The fifth diary contained only one item of note, apart from her conscientious record of the passing of the Reform Bill in June, 1832. She skipped over the year 1833 and passed on to November 30 1834 and the three words, 'William is dead'. What memories that evoked. Her long-delayed marriage to William of Gloucester had brought her nothing but misery. Apart from a few years of desultory service in the navy, William had done little of note when he married her, and by that time he was already a confirmed tippler. Nasty in his cups as George had put it. William had always been cruel to her, especially when he was more than usually befuddled with wine. Once he had struck her, knocking her down, and she had recalled with some longing the days when she and her sisters were shackled to Mama and sewing piebald pop-overs in the Gothic pavilion. Oh, how happy those days had seemed when compared with her present miserable existence. So she had been glad when he died, and not even conventional sorrow had been expressed in her diary.

Mary trimmed the wick of the candle before she embarked upon the sixth diary, for she wanted to have a good light by which to read it. This was her happy book, the one in which so many joyful events had been noted and re-read a thousand times. The single sombre note had been the death of her brother William, but that had been followed, of course, by Vicky's accession, and Vicky had been so kind to her. After her Coronation, which the Queen had regarded with some levity and a few childish complaints about the heaviness of the regalia, she had offered her aunt a home. Mary remembered her exact words, 'Come and live with me, Aunt. I cannot bear to think of you all alone in that *ugly* house of yours.' She had added with a smile, 'I shall not ask Aunt Augusta. She has her Brigadier to keep her company, nor shall I ask Aunt Sophie, for I believe she has an occasional visitor, too.' Mary had wondered how the sheltered Vicky, whose mother had not allowed the wind to blow on her, had come by this knowledge. It was true, of course. After the death of Mama, Sophie's 'lover' had retired and began to visit her quite openly. In 1840 Vicky had married Albert, after falling in love at the first sight of his handsome face and 'erect bearing'. In 1840, too, their first child had been born, Victoria Adelaide Mary Louisa. How very fertile Vicky was! Oh, she'd forgotten. She flicked back several pages. Her 'happy' book contained details of the death of Augusta and Elizabeth. Again, Elizabeth's death had not affected her much. She had not seen her for many years. As for Augusta, she had been so absorbed with her Brigadier that she had had little time to spare for her sisters.

Two diaries remained. 1842 — the birth of Albert Edward, Prince of Wales; 1843 — her brother Augustus died; 1848 — Sophie died, after eating tainted fish; 1850 — her brother Adolphus died.

Mary drew a long, heavy sigh. Her diaries were a saga of births, marriages and deaths, a record covering forty years. It was strange, she thought, how her life had been divided into two distinct halves. The first half had ended with her marriage and the death of Charlotte. The second half was ending with the birth of Beatrice. Yes, it would end soon, she knew. She was getting senile.

She rummaged around in the drawer again and pulled out a slip of yellowed paper which curled inward at the edges. It was a marriage certificate. Better burn it now. It could hurt Vicky terribly if she found it.

AUTHOR'S NOTE

On April 30 1857, Mary, Duchess of Gloucester, last surviving child of George III and Charlotte-Sophia of Mecklenburg-Strelitz, died at the age of eighty-five. Her life, and that of her niece the Princess Beatrice, spanned a period of one hundred and sixty-eight years, a period which began with the American Declaration of Independence and ended with the dropping of flying bombs on England by the Germans in World War II.

Other titles in the Linford Romance Library

SAVAGE PARADISE
Sheila Belshaw

For four years, Diana Hamilton had dreamed of returning to Luangwa Valley in Zambia. Now she was back — and, after a close encounter with a rhino — was receiving a lecture from a tall, khaki-clad man on the dangers of going into the bush alone!

PRETTY MAIDS ALL IN A ROW
Rose Meadows

The six beautiful daughters of George III of England dreamt of handsome princes coming to claim them, but the King always found some excuse to reject proposals of marriage. This is the story of what befell the Princesses as they began to seek lovers at their father's court, leaving behind rumours of secret marriages and illegitimate children.

A DREAM OF HER OWN
Barbara Best

A stranger gently kisses Sarah Danbury at her Betrothal Ball. Little does she realise that she is to meet this mysterious man again in very different circumstances.

HOSTAGE OF LOVE
Nara Lake

From the moment pretty Emma Tregear, the only child of a Van Diemen's Land magnate, met Philip Despard, she was desperately in love. Unfortunately, handsome Philip was a convict on parole.

THE GOLDEN GIRL
Paula Lindsay

Sarah had everything — wealth, social background, great beauty and magnetic charm. Her heart was ruled by love and compassion for the less fortunate in life. Yet, when one man's happiness was at stake, she failed him — and herself.

THE ROAD TO BENDOUR
Joyce Eaglestone

Mary Mackenzie had lived a sheltered life on the family farm in Scotland. When she took a job in the city she was soon in a romantic maze from which only she could find the way out.

THE VAUGHAN PRIDE
Margaret Miles

As the new owner of Southwood Manor, Laura Vaughan discovers that she's even more poverty stricken than before. She also finds that her neighbour, the handsome Marius Kerr, is a little too close for comfort.

HONEY-POT
Mira Stables

Lovely, well-born, well-dowered, Russet Ingram drew all the men to her. Yet here she was a prisoner of the one man immune to her graces accused of frivolously tampering with his young ward's romance!